DIRTY LOVE

AINSLEY BOOTH

WWW.AINSLEYBOOTH.COM

ABOUT THIS BOOK

WARNING: THIS IS JUST THE START. THIS DOESN'T END WELL.
AND IT'S GOING TO GET MUCH WORSE BEFORE IT EVER GETS
BETTER.

SOUND FAMILIAR? WELCOME TO THE NEXT STORY ABOUT THE
HORUS GROUP...

Wilson:

Tabitha Leyton is a mess, but now she's my mess.

To the rest of the world, she's a superstar.

Secretly, she's a witness to depravity and a train wreck waiting to happen.

But I can't get her out of my head. And for one angry, secret night, we have each other in every imaginable way.

The whole time, I know she's off-limits.

So in the morning, I'll walk away. Officially.

This is a standalone novel set in the Forbidden Bodyguards series. If you've read Hate F*@k, this book begins in the middle of that story, but extends far past it.

Some relationships are...complicated.

As always, all characters and events are fictional. And fucked up.

Any similarities to any real life people or events are entirely coincidental.

~ Ainsley

www.ainsleybooth.com

For everyone who's ever felt alone.

Dirty Love

part one

dirty whispers

[1]

WILSON

I'M DRIVING my beater truck that's just for nights like tonight, but I still park a few blocks from the warehouse.

Some guys might think that's foolish. They can't run as fast as I can. They don't fight as dirty as I do.

And they don't know what it's like to be trapped.

I'm never going to be trapped again.

I always know where my out is, even if it means I have to run like the wind for a few blocks to get to the car—but it won't be boxed in down an alley.

I check my phone before I head inside. She has a concert in San Francisco tonight. Won't go on stage for another thirty minutes.

Which means I have nearly three hours to beat the living shit out of anyone idiotic enough to try and take my money.

Then I'll want to make sure she gets back to her hotel safely. Not that I can do anything from the other side of the country, but this is the deal we've settled on.

For now.

My gut twists.

That's fine. I'll use that impotent rage in the ring.

Ring. That's a civilized term. Inside this warehouse there's just a concrete floor, crowded with people. And the two assholes in the center of the swarm pound on each other until one of them drops to the ground or begs for mercy.

Unlike some, I grant it if they ask.

Not because I'm soft. I'm not. I'm black inside, and I believe more than most that violence has its place. But I'm no longer a ghost, a secret shadow gliding through society. I have a business now, and partners, and doing the right thing makes sense for more than one reason.

Work, yes.

And now Tabitha as well.

Although when it comes to the woman I love, doing the right thing means doing a lot of wrong things first. She struggled with that at first, because she's innocent to the true darkness in the world. For all that she's done and experienced, she—like ninety-nine percent of the population—has no idea of what churns beneath the surface.

Her resistance didn't stop me. I've carefully been sliding domino pieces into place so when she's ready, when she's *safe*, I can push the first one and watch the chain reaction free her from her bonds.

Free her for the taking.

And until that point, I'll fight.

For Tabitha.

For justice, of a sort.

And sometimes, just because it feels fucking good to smash my fist into things.

"Fight! Fight! Fight!" The chanting crowd echoes what's inside me as I make my way inside. I catch the eye of the organizer and give him a brusque nod.

Yeah, I'm here. Bring on all challengers.

But first there's another pair of contenders in the ring. I unzip my hoodie and roll my neck, my shoulders. Bounce on my toes and start to move through some range of motion shit as I watch them move around each other.

They're both too cautious. The big guy will probably win. Everything else being equal, that's usually the way it goes. Might makes right.

The smaller guy is fast, though. If he got over his fear, he'd be worth putting money on.

If.

But that's the thing. What might happen if you get your shit together doesn't help you here, in the now, with some big guy's fist barrelling toward your jaw.

Sorry, bud. Not your night.

As the winner collects his earnings, I'm introduced. My fighting name is Nix, and it means absolutely nothing to me, like any of the other personas I put on to get a job done.

I'm Gough—pronounced Goff—when I'm impersonating an FBI agent.

Branch when I'm on the dark web.

Even Wilson Carter isn't a real name, but I made a choice six years ago. A choice to step into the light, to work with Mack Evans and now his half-brother Jason, and be a real person—as much as possible for someone like me.

And Wilson is as close to my real identity as I'm ever going to get.

Plus there's the fact Tabitha whispers that name when she comes. That would imprint it on my skin even if time and normalcy hadn't already done most of the work for her.

Tabitha.

Fucking hell.

I summon the rage that always simmers right beneath the surface and step forward, into the ring.

Bring it on, bastards.

[2]
TABITHA

Tonight's show was great. Long, though, with two extra encores, and I'm wiped. There's a girl backstage who's been shooting me looks, like she'd like to help me burn off some of this excess energy.

I think of him. Of how long it's been. Months since we last touched, since he's been inside me. Since we fucked, over and over again.

Since he imprinted himself on my skin and inside my soul.

A little black, bitter mark.

Nothing romantic about it.

But it's changed me, because I should want this girl. On her knees, between my legs. Her cute little pink tongue flicking at my clit, and an evil little part of my soul whispers it would be within the bounds of what he'd allow. She wouldn't fuck me. I wouldn't fuck her. Just a little taste.

But there's that mark. I'm his, for better or for worse.

And when I bump into her, and she spontaneously hugs me, there's no leap of hunger inside me. No shift into primal sex mode. I don't want her, not really. I want to not be so fucking lonely it hurts, but I don't want her. I don't want a stranger.

I want him.

I want the darkness, I want the demands. I want him again, like I had until I pushed him away. Hard and commanding and ruthless.

And unexpectedly principled.

That part was seriously inconvenient.

The girl is still lingering next to me. I brush my fingertips over her cheek. "You want me to introduce you to someone in the band, honey?"

She blushes, then looks up at me from under the world's longest, thickest eyelashes. "I really wanted to meet you."

Oh, sweet pea. No you don't. "I'm tired," I whisper. "But I bet Frankie would love to show you around."

She shrugs. Maybe she's only into girls.

Too bad for her. I'm taken, and by more than one man, although only one matters.

One night, and he stole my soul.

A few months, and he took my heart, too.

I always thought I was safe from something as mundane as love, that my heart was broken beyond repair. And in the end, I wasn't wrong. I'm as dysfunctional as they come.

And still he wants me.

"What are you thinking about?" The girl slides back into my bubble, presses against me, and now I'm starting to get annoyed.

"What's your name?"

She gives me a little smile. "Whatever you want it to be."

I roll my eyes. "I want it to be 'Yes, please, introduce me to Frankie. Or Ginger.'"

"Okay, I get the hint. Can't blame a girl for trying, right?"

I kiss her cheek. "Not at all. And another time, you'd be exactly my type." Another time, another year.

"Ginger...maybe."

"Good choice. She likes to party." I link my fingers through hers and wave at my back up singer.

It isn't a rule that everyone on my tour has to be depraved, but normal folks don't stick around.

"Tell you what, honey. If you and Ginger hit it off, I'll watch."

[3]

WILSON

I PARK in the alley behind the Tabard Inn and grab the bag of
ice from the passenger seat as I do a quick check on my video
feed of Tabitha. She's back at the hotel and there's a party in her
suite, as usual.

Fuck, the ice is cold as hell. But I'm not going to get its
numbing help again for a few hours, so I take a minute and
pretend my knuckles don't hurt like a motherfucker.

That third guy had a jaw of granite. Still took him down, of
course.

I take them all down.

Nix. Thirty-two wins. Zero loses. A legend in the underground circuit, even though he only makes an appearance a few
times a year.

Not my fault I've got real shit to do the rest of the time.

There's no real parking back here in the alley, but Mack
Evans owns the building I'm in front of, a few doors down from
the legendary Dupont Circle watering hole. A place where

people come to have important conversations. Close to international embassies and offices of lobbyists. Fixers, too, like The Horus Group.

Jason Evans, Cole Parker, Tag Browning and me. Wilson Carter. Funded at first by Jason's half-brother, Mack, a New York billionaire, and now...well, we're doing okay on our own, because we're the best at what we do. Crisis management, security.

Fighting like pit bulls, figuratively and literally.

And that's why I'm here tonight.

We have it on good authority there will be a meeting here tomorrow night. A popular white nationalist leader, Spencer Rook, will be holding court—that's not a secret. He's blogged about it and is practically taunting the media to come and cover him drinking whiskey and spouting bullshit in the same wing-back chairs senators and lobbyists relax in.

But in a private room upstairs, there will be another meeting. One he'll either duck into after he holds court, or maybe be a part of beforehand.

A shadowy international organization—that at one point hired our firm before we told them to fuck right off—has an interest in Rook. They'll be using him, or working with him, to make plans.

We need to know what those plans will be.

My job tonight is to get in and out of every private meeting space in the building and leave it bugged in an undetectable way.

I have everything I need stashed in the pockets of my leather jacket. Micro transmitters, filament sound recorders, impossibly small fish-eye cameras. I fucking love tech. Wiring a space used to be complicated. Now I can do it in as much time as it takes to fake a sneeze and tap my hand against the wall.

Inside, I move like a man looking for someone. A date, maybe, or more likely a business acquaintance. I want everyone who sees me to recognize my movements as ordinary and forgettable. I want to be seen and forgotten. The mind's ability to erase ordinary data is my biggest advantage. Even men who know me will see me approach Deacon Webb at the bar and have a drink with him, and assume we're old friends catching up.

Operating inside expectations is an excellent way to disguise unexpected behavior.

Friends isn't exactly how I'd describe my relationship with the secret service agent. Acquaintances with a shared mission at times is more like it. But nobody knows that. More to the point, nobody cares.

"You're back in town," I say, sliding on to the barstool next to him.

He gives me a sideways glance. "I've been recalled from the Los Angeles office. The service is going to have to bloat up for six months, remember?"

I make a face and he laughs. I hate politics. "Is it an election year?"

"Fuck off." He grins and waves over the bartender. "You here to meet someone?"

"Just finished a meeting," I lie. "I've got time for a drink."

I met Deacon at the CIA. He wasn't there long. The Secret Service detail is more his speed, and he doesn't know most of the levels on which I operated. He's not dense—not at all. He knew me first as Branch, but accepts my new Wilson identity with ease. Nobody does that without some context. But he's a genuinely good guy, driven by a noble sense of purpose.

We offered Deacon a job when we started up. He just laughed. He likes Homeland Security, although he's never been a fan of the presidential security part of the role. Financial crimes are his specialty.

"How long do you think you'll be around?" I take a long, slow sip of a top-shelf vodka. I'd gotten used to having him in the L.A. office. It had been helpful for my purposes.

"Just up until the election." His jaw flexes and I run down the list of candidates declared for both political parties that might need Secret Service protection at this point. I hate politics —that doesn't mean I don't follow them closely. His reaction and the timeline point to one strong possibility.

Deacon's going to be on the security detail for billionaire Victor Best.

Fucking hell. This is better than him being in the financial crimes office. I take another slow sip.

"Spit it out," Deacon growls under his breath.

"He's got interesting friends." Friends I've investigated. Friends I've set up and taken down.

"We're aware."

"Isn't he going to be deposed in the Gerome Lively case?" Sex crimes, human trafficking, kidnapping...the list of crimes that Lively's going to be pinned with is lengthy. Cole and Hailey had a lot to do with nailing that bastard to the wall.

"Not if his lawyers have anything to say about it." Deacon's voice is tight, clipped. "Nothing changes our responsibility to keep him safe as a potential candidate for the highest office in the land."

"Nice speech. That detail starting soon?"

He slugs back the rest of the amber liquid in his glass. "Immediately."

This complicates things. All of a sudden, PRISM takes a back seat to another plan I've already set in motion.

I hadn't counted on the Secret Service.

He watches me for a second, then changes the subject. "Haven't seen you in L.A. recently."

Tabitha's been on tour. "Work has kept me here."

"Do we have you to thank for some of the recent flags coming out credit unions in the south east?"

Yes. "I don't know what you're talking about."

"Good, because meddling in a federal investigation is a bad idea."

I snort. "Without hackers helping you behind the scenes, you'd be hamstrung by laws that lag twenty years behind technology."

"We'll nominate you for a congressional Medal of Honor, then."

"That would be awkward. I wouldn't be able to attend the ceremony."

"Still have a restraining order that keeps you off the Hill?"

I laugh. "Just allergic to the spotlight."

"Your partners aren't."

No, they'd really turned around on that front. I don't mind at all. That's convenient cover for me. But I'm not joining them as social crusaders. "Feel free to arrange some commendation for them on my behalf."

"That's above my pay grade."

We finish our drinks in silence, then I excuse myself to take a piss.

I head upstairs. In one room, a group is singing happy birthday. I hit the parlour across the hall first. It's empty. Takes me ten seconds to set up the first bug, then I stride across the room to do another. Two per room is my goal. Might only get one in the room with the birthday party, we'll see.

I work methodically, moving room to room. I don't skip the bathroom, either. Good conversations had there.

Finally I circle back to the birthday group. A waiter

approaches with a stack of plates, and I hold the door open for her.

"Thank you," she says gratefully.

No, thank you, I think to myself as I follow her in. The first bug goes on the door, facing the room. Then I do a quick scan. I don't know anyone in here. This can go two ways—either everyone will assume I'm with someone else, or they'll all know I'm an outsider who doesn't belong.

I can roll with either of those scenarios, but it's better if I can anticipate which I'll encounter. Do they look like they're all intimate friends? Or are some separated by more than one degree? Small, clustered conversations. The guest of honor is bobbing her head back and forth between two zones, trying to stay in two conversations at the same time.

They don't all know each other. I'm sure of it.

I move past the waiter, acting like I belong. Maybe I'm a manager or a date of a guest. In my head I'm working up a cover story as I do a quick visual check of the far wall. There's a thermostat. Perfect. I stride to it confidently, notch the heat down a few degrees, leave a bug, and flash a smile at the guests nearest as I do so. "Getting hot in here."

They laugh and say it sure is.

And I'm done.

I rejoin Deacon at the bar.

"Long line for the bathroom?" he asks, swirling a new drink around in his glass.

"Had to go upstairs."

"This place is crazy some nights."

Some more than others. I still need to get into the guest rooms, but I'll do that tomorrow morning when the maids are cleaning. "Good place to see and be seen, though."

He snorts. "Then why are we here?"

It was a good question. Why was he here?

This is thing about friendship when you're in my line of business. You can't truly trust anyone. Everyone is hiding something. Everyone has an agenda. Two. More. Agendas inside ideologies studded with debts and expectations and tied up with so many strings...

Washington. Fucking cesspool. And to think that when I moved here, I thought it was magical.

[4]

TABITHA

HE CALLS A LITTLE AFTER MIDNIGHT, Pacific time. Three in the morning for him. One ring, then he hangs up. A signal for me to call back once I'm alone.

I shoo everyone out of my suite, telling them I need to get some sleep.

Instead, I pick up the bottle of tequila I've been drinking from and head into my room, heart pounding.

He answers on the first ring, his voice chill and laid-back as always. "Have a good show?"

I hate small talk. "It was fine."

He doesn't reply right away. I don't want to talk about the tour, or performing. Also off-limits are discussions about my manager, my label, and why I've refused to see Wilson for almost four months.

We have this. That has to be enough for now.

I take a deep breath. "What did you do tonight?"

He laughs. "Knocked the shit out of assholes for money."

"That's healthy."

Ignoring my sarcasm, he drops his voice. Less chill, more intense. "I want you to come watch me fight some time."

"I've been to fights in Vegas. I hate them."

"What I do isn't like anything you'd see in Vegas, secret girl."

Oh, it's going to be that kind of night. Someone's horny, and he knows the pet name gets me going despite myself. I roll onto my side. "I'd go and watch." This is our shared, impossible fantasy. It makes my chest ache. "Tell me about it."

I picture him prowling into a dark industrial park. Hoodie up, slim sweatpants. He'd look like a teenage punk. I asked him once how old he is. He doesn't look like he's in his mid-thirties, but he swears his baby face is more of a curse than a blessing.

He obviously hasn't spent enough time in Hollywood.

"So there's some waiting around, watching the other fights," he says, still setting the scene for me.

"Is it dangerous?"

"Do you want it to be?"

I press my thighs together. "I want you to stand between me and danger."

"I do."

"I know." I take a deep breath because we've drifted out of the fantasy and into reality. I hate reality. "How many people?"

"A hundred, maybe. Tonight there weren't that many. Only a handful of dates, no big rollers in person."

"In person? Where else...is this filmed?" My heart starts to pound.

"Live steamed to interested parties that pay top dollar for access."

"You aren't worried about that?"

"I don't worry about anything."

I know that. I still don't believe it, but I understand he does. "*I* worry."

"That's the sweetest thing you've ever said to me."

His voice wraps around me, pressing into my skin. The words prick into me like thorns—and I like the sharp pierce a little too much. I need to get this back on track. "What would I wear to this fight of yours?"

"Whatever you want."

"But if you could dress me?"

He grunts, a rough, guttural noise that makes me squirm. "Jean skirt. Short. Black tank top."

What I'm wearing.

"And a leather jacket to keep you warm. No bra."

"Panties?"

"A thong. Easy to pull aside."

"And would you?"

Another noise, this one more helpless and in the back of his throat. This is what he called me for. My brazen, no-limits phone sex. My total and utter depravity.

"Would you finger me while I watch two men pummel each other? Would you go into your own fight with my come on your fingers, leaving me shaking and helpless at the sidelines?"

"I wouldn't leave you alone."

"Who would hold me? Who would you trust?"

"I don't trust anyone." And that's the thing, isn't it...we're alone in this together. Us against the world, trusting no-one. "I'd bring a guard."

"Would he touch me?"

"Never."

"Even if I wanted him to?" This is cruel of me. I know he's possessive. I know he hates that I'm off-limits, claimed by another. But he knows that I'm all his in the only way that matters.

"You don't." His voice shifts. Heavier, more demanding.

"You don't want anyone else's fingers on your clit. Inside you. That's my responsibility. My pleasure."

"Yes," I breathe, sliding my hand down my body. I'm wearing a jean skirt now. Short. I flick my gaze to the corner of the room where my traveling wardrobe is set up. Where at least one of Wilson's cameras is carefully hidden. "Are you watching?"

"Always."

"Where are you?" It's not fair that he can see me and I can't see him.

"At home. Spread your legs."

"I'm not wearing a thong," I tease. I'm not wearing anything, and I know he can see that when I slide my legs apart.

"Dirty girl."

"Always."

"Don't steal my lines. What were you doing before you called?"

Eight months ago, I'd have been having sex with half of my crew. Tonight, and every night since Wilson claimed me, I just watched the usual debauchery that spilled out after a show. "There was the usual thing. I'm surprised you don't know."

"I was busy."

It's nearly three in the morning on the east coast. "Fights went late?"

"I had a thing after that. Touch yourself. I want to see your fingers slide inside."

I stroke myself, the outer lips first, then where I'm wet already. I lift my hips and give in to the memory of his fingers spearing into me. Roughly, before I'm ready, because I goaded him into it.

"Slow down," he says in my ear, and I make a face that makes him laugh. "Put me on speaker so you can use both hands."

"I like having your voice right in my ear." To prove my point, I show him I only need one hand. I'm a masturbating ninja.

"Keep saying nice things to me and I'm going to think you want another visit."

"Want and can handle are two different things." I pull my hand from between my legs and give him my middle finger. "Your voice makes me wet, nothing else. I like it for depraved reasons."

"You want a bedtime story?"

I lick my finger and drag it back down my body, tugging at my tank top as I go. "Please."

"Once upon a time, there was a man who flew to a city of angels in search of answers."

Oh, that's a dirty trick, going with this story. My throat tightens even as the rest of my body goes soft and pliant for him.

Wilson holds the pause just long enough to make me ache. "He found a dark, dirty siren instead. She tempted him, and he fell hopelessly in lust with her."

The feeling had been completely mutual, the bastard. He'd twisted me inside out with a single look.

"But she lived in a tall tower, guarded by an ugly troll, and there was no way for him to get up, nor her to get down. So he found a way to send her messages instead. Dirty stories of all the filthy things he wanted to do to her. To her mouth. Her pussy. Her ass."

"Yes," I breathe. "Are you jerking yourself off?"

"Hush. Listen to your story. So one night, he found a way to talk to her. To tell her how much he wanted to taste her. To bury his face between her legs and lick her until she squirmed. And as he talked to her, she touched herself. She told him how soft and wet and perfect she was for him, and only him."

"I am. And only for you," I whisper. He really has made me a romantic in my own way.

I'm totally going to break his heart. The tightness in my throat moves into my chest. Whatever. My heart is already broken.

"Lemme hear you come," he says, his voice fading into a groan. I picture him squeezing his cock, tugging faster around the head, then backing off again. Edging himself because torture is all we've got.

Fuck. My entire torso's consumed with that heat now, the uncomfortable claiming, and I writhe, against it and toward it. My head thrashes away from the phone, and his voice is distant for a second, but then I twist back.

"Fill yourself up. Fuck yourself and imagine it's me." Rough, harsh commands. I close my eyes and my lips part. I can feel his fingers inside me, then wet against my thighs. My belly. His hand on my neck, a squeeze to make me gasp. Then he'd thrust his cock into me and I'd cry out. He'd silence me with his fingers, slick with the taste of me, and I'd suck on him because I'm a dirty fallen angel.

All for him, now.

How my life has changed.

[5]

WILSON

Dawn crawls though the bare, bulletproof windows of my loft, waking me up. In my dreams, I could smell Tabitha on my fingers, taste her on my tongue.

Now I lie in bed, angry and frustrated and impatient. This bullshit has gone on long enough. Fuck. Until I met her last summer, I didn't do emotional reactions—ever. And now I'm a caged tiger half the time, prowling because my mate's on the other side of the country and out of reach.

I'm protecting her, though. On her terms.

And I get it. She has a lot of people that depend on the life she leads. The business empire beneath her.

Being mine would threaten all of that.

I force myself out of bed. No more thinking about that. The wheels are in motion. I need to be patient.

I work out first. I'm sore from the fights last night, and it feels good to get blood flowing through my muscles again. Punching bag, pushups, situps. Repeat over and over again until I hear my programmed coffee maker hiss to life.

Shower.

Protein drink.

Coffee.

The office is empty when I arrive. We used to have a receptionist, but she up and quit unexpectedly, and we've never hired another one. That was Jason's call, and I don't care. I don't have clients that come to see me.

I'm the eyes and ears of The Horus Group. I watch our clients, their enemies, possible sources, and anyone else who crosses our path. I dig deep into backgrounds and identities, looking for patterns and disruptions.

Sometimes I'm a hacker, following the digital trail of criminals and politicians and businesses.

People hate politicians, and with good reason. Power is corrupting.

But big business is where the truly scary stuff is happening, because nobody's really watching. Sure, there are federal watch dogs, but the reality is, they're underfunded and staffed by people who think in terms of black and white. Right and wrong.

That's not how the business world works.

That's not how the richest of the rich think—at all. They genuinely think the rules are different for them, that they can operate with impunity and outside the law, because history has given them that ego.

Even the people who are made examples of are relatively "poor" compared to the chess masters. The puppeteers.

PRISM, for example. A shadowy extra governmental organization with unlimited funds and shadowy purpose.

We used to work for them.

Now...well, that's a bit in flux. Part of that is because of Cole's experience with his wife. He met Hailey when we were hired to get her father out of trouble—felony-level trouble.

Since he's a billionaire and we're good at our jobs, we did it handily. No more dead hooker. No problem.

I'm not so depraved that I didn't feel a little sick as we disposed of the body. But we had our orders—from PRISM.

We didn't find out that Hailey's mother is a PRISM stakeholder until much later.

Too late.

But we're going to make it right. Tonight is the first foray we're making into actively investigating them, and I'm stoked about it. Of course I am, I'm an adrenaline junkie.

It doesn't matter what the risk is, either. Physical harm, good. But hacking gives me the same kind of rush.

I log in to my systems. I've got a few different ones set up, all on different networks, routed through cloaking software. This morning I'm doing a couple of things. Running background on Victor Best is on the to-do list. We've got a dossier on everyone, including him, but I want to make sure it's complete. He'd slipped off my radar when he went political, because fringe candidates are usually whackos more intent on hearing their own voices than actually manipulating the process to get real results.

But if he's going to have Secret Service protection, he's got real credibility.

Something tells me this is bad fucking news.

I'm also running some bots in chat rooms. One of them is pretending to be a shy teenage girl. Another, a young man, early twenties, but willing to play younger than that for the right price. The artificial intelligence technology is changing daily, and I'm really pleased with how these bots are producing results. Some of the potential pedophiles catch on that something's not quite right, but that data is useful, too. I can train the AI bot to not use that kind of response again, whatever triggered the end of the conversation.

"Morning."

I glance sideways and nod at Cole. He's in a suit today. "Morning. Heading out?"

"Got a whistleblower client meeting with some agents at the DOJ in a few hours. What are you working on?"

I wave at the screen where the girl bot is playing it coy enough to make the idiot talking to her say something stupid. "The usual."

"Who is he?" Cole leans in and looks at the scrolling data. This is best and worst part of my job. While the bots are engaging, I'm tracing as much as I can from the digital footprint of the asshole on the other end. In this case, it's a firefighter in Florida who doesn't even know how to use a proxy server.

"A father of teenage boys. Twice divorced. Owns his house, but he's got some debt. Has bounced through a couple of fire departments. At the rate he moves through jobs, he might not be fun to work with. Anger issues, maybe. He's being aggressive with the bot. Pushing her."

Cole clenches his fist until his knuckles turn white. "Fucking endless."

"Yep. Get out of my office unless you want to see some shit you'll never un-see."

He steps back, but he doesn't leave. "Why did you meet with Deacon Webb?"

"Last night?"

"How many times have you met with him?"

I type a command into the dialog box on my screen and a new search script begins, looking for irregular cash withdrawals. Has he hired any hookers in real life? "I see Webb from time to time when I'm in L.A. Why?"

"You haven't mentioned that."

"I didn't realize I need to. How did you know we ran into each other last night?"

Cole doesn't say anything. The night's activities flash

through my mind like a slideshow. I hadn't seen him. I frown and spin around in my chair.

He's rubbing his jaw, but he's not avoiding my gaze. So it wasn't him, and it wasn't Tag, either. For one thing, Tag would have just come over. Stealth isn't his style. And for another, he doesn't always assume the worst of me. "Jason?"

Cole shrugs.

Sometimes we're fucking assholes to each other. I give him a hard look. "I went to drop the first round of wires. Jason knew that, there's no secret. I saw Webb at the bar, and stopped to have a drink with him. We talked about his work, mostly. Key question really is, why was Jason there—if he didn't come over and talk to me—and why isn't he having this conversation with me now?"

"He just mentioned it in passing."

"And now I'm flipping it back to you—in passing. What's Jason up to?"

Cole's jaw flexes. He's not entirely comfortable with the dark side of the moon our partner still sometimes drifts toward. Where we all started from, and most naturally operate.

I cross my arms. "Was I sent on a fool's errand last night? A diversion?"

"No." He frowns. "I'm more worried about you leaving. Forming your own firm with Webb."

"Ah, shit, man. No. Not going to happen. He's happy with the Secret Service. You know if anything I'd just try to get him here. I'm not looking to jump anywhere. Where is this coming from?"

He shifts back on his heels and crosses his arms, mirroring my pose. Except Cole's a beast, with arms the size of a well-fed python, so he's definitely the more intimidating of the two of us. Which makes it all the more disconcerting when he gives me a tentative smile. "I don't want you to think I've gone soft."

I shake my head. "Never. Not in the ways that matter." Sure, Cole fell hard for a good girl, but Hailey also lights a fire under him to do the right thing—and fuck it, I can hack for good just as well as evil. "But my conversation with Webb actually was productive...he's back in town to join the security detail designated for Victor Best."

Cole's smile disappears and his face turns dark. "Damn."

"Yeah. Looks like the Secretary for Homeland Security sees Best's presidential campaign as having some legs."

"The guy's total scum."

"Tell me about it. He's on the witness list for the civil case against Gerome Lively."

"Do we have a dossier on him?"

I point to my third screen. "Already updating it. Should have a complete picture of what he's been up to by the end of the day."

[6]

TABITHA

We hit the road a bit before noon. Next stop is Portland.

I thought last night's show had been awesome, but the ticket numbers Grant dumps silently in front of me show a different reality.

I knew we weren't sold out, but only seventy percent sold is...ouch. The promoter organizing this tour deliberately priced my tickets competitively, almost twenty bucks a pop less than my last tour. The attendance numbers hadn't jumped, making the deal a terrible business decision.

And now it looks like my manager is trying to pin that on me.

Fuck him.

There's a sticky note on top of the sales numbers, a reminder from Grant that I have a doctor's appointment for my quarterly B-12 shot in the morning. I pull it off and crumple it up. Jackass. I put all my appointments in my phone and I never miss any of them.

I look over the numbers, but I don't say anything. He fumes in the opposite seat for a few minutes, then gets up and goes up front where Frankie and some of the crew are watching a fight recorded from the night before.

The sounds drifting back in my direction made me think of Wilson.

I'd tried to say no. I'd tried to stop *us*, but there's no stopping *him*.

And even though I won't let him come and see me—it's too hard, too much, especially while I'm on tour—he's still where my mind goes.

Grant knows it. I don't know if he's pieced together the details, but it's not like it's any secret that Wilson doesn't like him.

Fucking hell. This is a nightmare, and one of my own making.

I don't like anyone at the label. Or any label for that matter. I've spent a decade burning bridges and flipping people off, so it's not like I've got allies if I wanted to break away from Grant. He holds everything together. I do my thing on stage and in the studio. That's the deal.

When he comes back, I'm halfway reconciled toward some kind of apology. I wouldn't mean it, and we'd both know that, but it's what I need to do to maintain the peace.

Except he doesn't want to talk about numbers first.

He wants to make my head explode.

This time, he doesn't sit across the aisle from me. He takes the seat right next to me, close enough for me to unwillingly catch a whiff of his aftershave. He's worn the same brand for ten years. It still makes me want to vomit.

He gives me a cool smile. His eyes are hard. "Victor Best will be in Portland tomorrow. He wants to come by and take a picture with you before the show."

Revulsion rises in my gut. Best is a part owner in the radio network that also owns the tour promoter. He famously hates the Pacific Northwest, and we hate him right back, although I suppose that doesn't mean he can never have any business there.

Being from the Seattle area myself, I know how people talk about him. How happy they were when he bought a place in Florida and loudly proclaimed he'd never come back to the Pacific Northwest. Too bad that didn't last.

He's crazy. And kind of gross. I've met him twice before, once in Los Angeles and once in Italy. He runs in the same circles as Gerome Lively, and the mention of him immediately makes me think of Wilson.

Of the first time I met him, and everything that has happened since then.

"Sure," I hear myself say to Grant. "How about we invite him backstage? I can..." I let my mouth twist into something that he'll see as a dirty offer, a smile of sin. "I can entertain him a little."

"He might have his wife with him."

I toss my hair. "Oh, kinky."

"Tabitha."

"What? Are you going to pretend you don't want me to blow him? You want me to blow everybody."

He doesn't say anything.

I close my eyes. "I need my rest. Go away. I'll do your bidding and you can judge me for it, just like always."

At first I think it's going to work. But then I feel the heat of his body, an oppressive blanket against my side. His words come out hissing like snake. "Don't you fuck with me, Tabitha. I know all your dirty secrets, and unless you want them plastered... everywhere, you'll keep your fucking mouth shut. And your legs, too."

We've done this before, many times. It never gets easier. I press my palms to my legs and will myself not to freak out. "I'm not—"

"Don't lie to me. You're...planning something." He draws an unsteady breath. I still don't look at him. "But you think you're just hurting me. Ticket sales are slow for the next tour leg. You're fucking this up for everyone."

I know I am. I start to shake. "It's all your fault," I whisper. Fuck it. Fuck him. I don't care anymore.

He laughs, close enough to my face that I feel his breath against my cheek. It feels hot and gross. Drops of spit land on my cheek as I turn away. "You've always got another choice, Tabitha. Ten years and you haven't taken it."

"Not much of a choice."

"Only because you're a pathetic, greedy bitch." Hard and heavy, his words bludgeon me. Slam. You're awful. Slam. You're gross. Slam. You're a slut. Slam—

A song starts in the back of my mind. Darkness pulls in around me as I disconnect from his hatred, pulling into myself. I'm scared, yeah. Fucking petrified. But I've learned how to survive, too.

He has no idea.

No, I don't have a plan. Wilson's kept me deliberately in the dark. That doesn't mean I can't and won't defend myself if the opportunity presents itself.

And Victor Best in my dressing room? Maybe I can work with that. What's the worst that can happen?

Dirty Love

part one

dirty

[7]

WILSON

LOS ANGELES

JULY

I don't like L.A.

It's my job to sniff out insincerity, to figure out where the lies begin to stain the truth and trace the edges to the culprit. Because there's always someone pulling the strings. There's always a puppet master.

The problem is, in L.A., everyone's a puppet master, and life is a set of staged lies.

They call it performance.

I call it fucking annoying.

My partners don't care, which means I'm an idiot for volunteering to fly out for this interview.

There are four of us. Jason Evans and Cole Parker are ex-

Navy SEALs. Tag Browning is an ex-DC cop.

I'm ex-none-of-your-fucking-business. The hacker, the black-ops insider.

Together, we're The Horus Group, Washington's hottest crisis management firm.

And right now, I'm waiting in a suite at the Bel Air, watching the surveillance feed I set up earlier today on my phone. Jason is pacing. We're here to interview Tabitha Leyton, America's favorite singer-songwriter.

Former fuck toy of Gerome Lively, if I'm not mistaken.

We're investigating the billionaire for human trafficking. So is the FBI, but they're not getting anywhere. It's complicated as fuck and the further I climb into the dark underbelly of this world, the more I realize how messy it is.

In theory, we're here to interview Tabitha so she might be a witness at a trial against Lively—a trial I'm highly doubtful will ever take place.

Practically, we're here because I deal in information, and if I know something about this woman, there might be a time when I can use it.

And knowing *anything* about Tabitha Leyton is a minor miracle. She's shrouded in mystery, and not just to the public.

She's sex and secrets personified.

From the first time she pinged on my radar, she's had this effect on me. Unsettling. Taunting.

Her official identity is too clean. I haven't shared this with my partners, but I know Tabitha's hiding something. Many somethings, probably. It's a gut feeling, and I don't like to admit that I sometimes operate on instinct like that.

The door swings open, but it's not the woman we're waiting for. Instead it's her manager, Grant Derew. Formerly an agent, Derew found Tabitha at the age of fifteen in a small town in

Washington State and propelled her to stardom. Now he manages her full-time.

I instantly hate the guy. And he introduced Tabitha to Lively, so he's already a douchebag who's led around by his dick and a perverted desire for jailbait.

"Gentleman, I understand you had an appointment with Tabitha. Unfortunately—"

I ignore his outstretched hand, because fuck if I'm going to touch him. I shove to my feet. "We *have* an appointment, and we're going to keep it."

I stalk past him, through the front door of the suite. I've got a master room key in my pocket, and I use it to open the only other door on this floor.

She's on the other side.

My first in-person impression isn't what I expect.

She's both bigger and smaller than I pictured in my head. Big hair, big tits, big attitude. But the rest of her is surprisingly small, right down to the look in her eye.

She's scared.

She doesn't look it. Her eyes are burning at the invasion of her privacy, as they should. I'm an asshole. I work with other assholes, and we'll stop at nothing.

I'm going to steamroll right over her and she should be afraid of me.

Then her eyes flick past me, over my shoulder, and I turn slowly.

She's not afraid of me.

It's him. Derew.

One asshole knows another, and I give him a hard look, flashing my badge. He doesn't know it's as fake as the names I'm about to give. "Agents Gough and Weston. We need the room."

If he was smart—he's not—he'd have done more to vet this interview than looking us up on the FBI's public website.

Hacking that shit and putting our photos there for a few days was a kindergarten exercise. I watched someone from his office click on our page, then email him the link and say we were legit.

Fucking amateurs.

And we won't talk about how the feds didn't even notice my temporary takeover of their financial crimes division's website.

Jason strong-arms Derew out of the room, then we sit across from Tabitha. Oversized white leather couches, nothing like the room next door. I look around, taking it all in. Her guitar, complete with banged up case covered in the dreamer stickers of a teenage girl. Nearly a decade in the spotlight hasn't changed her hopes and dreams.

And clearly, she hasn't actually achieved them yet. I set my phone on the coffee table between us and lean forward, resting my elbows on my knees. I let my hair flop in front of my eyes a bit and give her an understanding look.

Women love this shit.

They have no clue that I'm dead inside, that I pummel other men to bloody pulps for sport and I've killed my enemies and then gone out for ice cream.

Mint chocolate chip cures all.

"Ms. Leyton," I start.

She cuts me off. "First of all, I don't believe you guys are feds. Second of all, there's nothing polite about me, so call me Tabitha or baby girl or nothing at all. Got it?"

No, I don't *got it*. What the fuck does she mean we don't look like feds?

I *was* a fucking fed. Not the FBI. Fuck that child's play. But I was one degree of Kevin Bacon away from the President of the United States of America for six years. I know how to wear this badge even if it wasn't given to me by a deputy director of national intelligence.

"Tabitha."

She gives me an arch look and I smirk. Does she think I'd call her baby girl?

My dick chubs up and she smirks right back. Fuck. I refuse to look at her painted red lips. I hold her gaze and return my expression to cold disinterest. "We don't need to call you anything. We're just here to find out what your financial connection is to Gerome Lively."

"Uhhh..." Her mouth drops open and while she's busy flicking her eyes to the right—liar, liar, pants on fire—I take a mental picture of those parted lips, that pink tongue, the hint of pearly white teeth.

My cock shoving into her mouth and her startled cry of surprise.

Fuck. Me.

I never do this. I never mix business and pleasure, because my brand of pleasure isn't acceptable for public consumption. I force myself to think of computer code. Command prompts and dial-up connections. I drag myself back to being that skinny-assed kid who was sure he'd never get laid, so he spent too much time deep in the dark corners of the Internet learning about the wrong kind of sex.

"What did you think we were here to discuss, Ms. Leyton?"

She scowls at Jason, but she doesn't tell him to call her baby girl. "I have no clue."

"But you do know Mr. Lively."

"Sure. He's loaded. I know a lot of rich people." She flips her hair over her shoulder—dark red hair, porcelain skin. She's like a fucking doll. A bratty doll that needs to be spanked until she screams, which isn't even my thing. I don't like games. I like a soft pair of tits and a sweet ass, a wet mouth and zero back talk—and if all of the above can come in a guaranteed-to-be-anonymous and doesn't-mind-being-railed-in-the-ass package, all the better.

Tabitha fails on at least two of the six points.

Her tits are spectacular, though.

And that mouth.

I stand up.

Her gaze follows me.

Good. I've got her attention. "Can you tell us about a trip you took in August, two years ago, to the Florida Keys?"

She frowns. "No?"

"No?"

"I didn't go to Florida two years ago in August."

Yes she did. "You sound awfully sure of that."

"I was supposed to. I had a concert in NOLA the night before." She gives me a faint smile, one that says *ha* and *no, I won't tell you more* at the same time. "And then I...didn't."

"Where did you go instead?"

"Fargo."

There was no trace of that. "How?"

"Private plane."

"No flight plan was registered."

She crosses her arms. "No."

"That's a federal offense."

"I wasn't flying the plane."

"But you were aware at the time that you were heading in the opposite direction of your cell phone, your passport, and your entire entourage?"

"Yes."

"Why?"

"Why was I aware? Because I'm a sentient being," she snaps, her green eyes blazing. I can feel Jason watching me, going, *what the fuck, man?* I never lose my cool, and it's gone now.

I spit out the next question. "Why did you go out of your

way to make it appear like you spent a weekend with Gerome Lively, when really you went to…"

"Fargo." She waits.

I wait longer.

Jason finally interrupts. "Ms. Leyton, have you ever met Gerome Lively?"

The tip of her tongue peeks out the corner of her mouth. Thinking. She glances up at the ceiling, then rolls her bottom lip between her teeth. "Yes," she finally admits.

"How many times?"

"Once."

He frowns at me. My research is rarely wrong. I have four visits, based on information I've cobbled together from her passport, her cell phone history, and commercial flight data. A week on a yacht in the Mediterranean, the phantom weekend to his estate in the Florida Keys, one trip to his private island in the Caribbean, and they definitely attended the same fundraiser here in L.A., hosted by a big-name movie producer.

"Tabitha," I say quietly. Might as well cut to the chase. "Did Gerome Lively rape you?"

[8]

TABITHA

I SHOULDN'T HAVE TOLD him to call me Tabitha. It's way too intimate. It was supposed to knock him off his game, not give him a weapon against me.

I don't know who these guys are or what they want, but no way am I answering that question. I don't trust sincerity, I don't trust badges, I don't trust men. Three strikes and you're out.

The muscle-bound one who doesn't talk much gives his friend a warning look that the blond guy completely ignores. I guess he just went off script.

Good. That means that I'm in charge now, and that's exactly how I like it.

"Rape me?" I roll my eyes even as my stomach twists uncomfortably. "I thought this was about money."

He looks at me, his gray eyes shifting back and forth like he's trying to figure me out. Like I'm a puzzle and if he moves the pieces around long enough, they'll fall into place.

Well, joke's on him. I'm missing half of the pieces that would make me whole. No matter how long he stares at me, I'm still going to look like a Rorschach test—maybe something you can make sense of if you squint, but in reality just a splatter stain.

"It is." He shifts forward onto the balls of his feet, then back onto his heels. He's thinking.

I roll my eyes. "Okay, well, it was fun watching you shove my manager out of the suite, but before I call hotel security and have you kicked out for trespassing, I'm going to ask you to leave. Nicely."

"You want us to leave nicely?" He crooks one eyebrow. *Wanna dance, little one?*

He knows what I meant. I ignore the petulant whine that rises in my chest. "Yes, please."

"Make you a deal. Tell us more than yes/no answers about your relationship with Lively—financial, sexual, etcetera—and we'll leave super nicely."

"No can do, *sir*." I stand and move toward the phone. "I don't have a *relationship* with him, so there's nothing to elaborate on."

"We're not done here." His words tug at my insides. Oh yeah, we are.

"I have a show to get ready for tonight, unfortunately. And my vocal coach insists I don't use my voice for six hours before a performance, so..." I shrug.

His eyes glitter, just for a second, then he blinks and it's gone. Emotion...poof. That's a neat trick. I'd love to be able to do that without a bottle of tequila or a pile of naked bodies.

"What time is your show?" He glances at his watch, then back at me. Bland again.

I don't like that.

I don't like this interview, I don't like him, I don't like being put in this position where *my* life is exposed because Grant wanted to play Lifestyles of the Rich and Perverted six years ago.

One time. That's all I put up with.

Don't get me wrong, I don't mind an orgy. Only way I have sex. But there's no way those girls had consented to be there.

I don't really get it. There are plenty of us sluts to go around —why the hell verge into criminal behavior to get your rocks off?

I live my life on the edge of the law, and nobody knows it. I'm sure as hell not going to recklessly wander across that line just for a dirty fuck.

Those are as easy to come by as apple-fucking-pie. I could have one with these two wannabe-cops right now.

"I asked you a question," the blond one repeats and his friend mutters something I don't catch. Frankly, I'd forgotten the other guy was in the room until my mind turned to sex.

Safety in numbers, that's my motto.

And suddenly I realize that this bitchiness is because I want this guy. The blond one. Agent Asshole. I want him on his knees, licking my pussy and calling me ma'am.

There is nothing I like better than bringing grown men to heel.

"Tabitha." His voice is unreal. Quiet, steely, and commanding. I jerk my shoulders back. "We're not here to expose you. We're strictly interested in understanding more about how Lively operates—the financial side, and yes, the sexual violence."

"Why?"

He stills, and I look back and forth between the two of them. He's not usually in charge, I decide. Why he's taking the lead here, I'm not sure. Maybe this is his investigation. But the other guy is watching him carefully.

'The nature of the investigation is confidential," he finally answers.

"Well, then so is the nature of my knowledge, should I have any. Which I don't." I stand up, and I don't miss how his eyelids drop just a hair, just enough to mask that he's looking at me. Tracing down my body, then back up again, and his gaze lingers on my hips. My tits.

Fucking men. So easily swayed.

He wants to see my tits? Happy to oblige. I cross my hands at my waist and grip the bottom of my tank top. The other guy curses under his breath as I slide the cotton fabric up my torso, over my head, and let it fall on the ground.

"Like I said, I can't talk anymore this afternoon, but my vocal coach doesn't have any rules about other uses for my mouth." I wink at the blond one and turn around, denying him the view of my chest. But before I lose his attention, I undo the heavy leather belt that decorates the top of my hip hugger jeans and shove those to the ground.

The other one is staring at the ceiling now. That won't do.

"You," I purr. He looks at me. Good, he's not embarrassed. I don't have any time for chivalry, either, but it's more easily worked around than nerves.

Nothing worse than a guy coming in his pants before I get my mouth on him.

"What's your name, really?"

"Kevin Weston."

I laugh. "And what's your friend's name?"

From behind me—closer than I expect—I hear the voice of steel again. "Wilson...Gough."

Ah. "Wilson," I say, blinking at him over my shoulder. Shit, he's tall. Like a foot taller than me, and big. And he smells like he'd taste *amazing*. Asshole.

I can hear my therapist in my head. It's not this guy's fault that he's hot. That I'm fucked up and use sex as a replacement for everything in my life.

Better than tequila, I usually joke.

Dr. Yost really hates jokes.

I think Wilson's not big on them either. He glares down at my half-naked body, then back at my face again. "This stunt isn't convincing me that you're unaffected by your encounters with Gerome Lively, Tabitha."

"Should I give your friend a blow job, Wilson?" I lick my lips as I ask the question, loving the way the tension in the room ratchets up a thousand degrees. Welcome to my world, men. Where I finally have an advantage because fucked-up is my life, my every day, so now that you're off-kilter, I can forge ahead and seize the upper hand. "That's what I asked Lively, by the way, the one time I spent any time with him. He looked me up and down and told me that he'd like to split me in two. I slid my hands into his pants and told him I prefer to be split in three, and he'd need a friend to help."

Blink.

That's all I get. I'm supposed to get red faces and stammering apologies. Offers of trauma counselling and kind words about how none of it is my fault.

Instead I get a whisper that cuts me to the quick. "My friend *is* a bit tense," Wilson murmurs, his eyes strangely warm. Not like he thinks I'm kidding—there's a scary edge there that says, no, he knows exactly what goes on with Lively's parties and he believes that exchange really happened. But he's not going to let me shock my way out of this conversation.

Well, I'm not backing down, either. I spin, then sway my way toward *Kevin*. Definitely not his name. Wilson's pupils dilate when I say his name. This guy is cold and hard like granite. I reach behind me and unclasp my bra, then hold on to the cups in the front so it doesn't fall away. Not for modesty—I don't have any—but because the lure of what they can't see is so much more powerful than what they can.

I get as far as reaching for his belt before he steps back, and I wobble, catching myself from falling onto all fours.

Then I hear it. A catch in Wilson's throat, maybe. A groan of the quietest order.

And I drop to my hands and knees, pressing my ass in the air.

"Ms. Leyton, we'll let you get ready for your performance now," *Kevin* says. I push back onto my knees and glance at Wilson, but he's already standing.

Walking around me.

Walking away from me, because I'm a fucked-up mess and was no use to them.

Exactly what I set out to do, but damn, it doesn't feel good.

Nothing about my life feels good outside the two hours I'm on stage, and I close my eyes, grateful that tonight I'll get to escape for a bit.

I start shivering as soon as the door clicks shut behind them. I don't even hear Grant come in a few minutes later.

"What did you tell them?"

I shake my head. "Nothing. Of course I told them nothing."

He sneers down at me. "I don't know. Sometimes you get these crazy ideas in your head."

"Well, I didn't today." I stand up and walk to the kitchenette, grabbing a robe from one of bar stools on my way. "Can you call the concierge and arrange for a massage therapist in an hour? I'm feeling tense."

He doesn't answer right away.

I yank open the fridge and grab a pre-made kale and pineapple smoothie. Mmm. Lunch. Fuck my life. "Okay, fine. I'll call myself. Or just watch porn and masturbate like regular people do."

"You don't need to be like that. I'm just wondering if it's wise—"

Fuck. He thinks I'm going to hit on the RMT they send up. He has no clue that the last person I fucked alone was him, ten years ago. I'll never make that mistake again. "Tell you what. I'll keep my hands to myself, okay?" An easy promise to make, seeing as how I never planned to violate the poor person in the first place.

He sighs, and for a second, I see the guy who discovered me. Who cared, a little too much and a lot too inappropriately, but he did care.

Now? Now we're tied together for life and it all rides on my ability to not fall apart. So I need a fucking massage, and he knows he needs to make that happen.

When he leaves again, I slump back against the kitchen counter and feel the almost-tears burning in the back of my eyes. They never fall.

I cried all the tears when I gave birth to my stillborn son, my baby, when I was fifteen.

Since then I've been on a slow-burning self-destruct sequence, and nothing will change that.

No well-meaning investigators from God knows where.

No massage.

No fucking kale and pineapple smoothie.

Not even a crowd of thousands of fans, all cheering my name as I belt out blistering song after blistering song about the cruelty of love.

If only they knew.

Jason pulls out his phone as soon as we're back in our suite.

"What are you going to tell them?" If it hadn't been trained out of me, I'd be breathing hard right now. Inside, my pulse is racing and my mind is swirling with the imagined scent of her and the coppery taste of regret that I have to make something up, that she didn't get close enough for me to know.

"Not about the wood you popped at the thought of me getting a blow job from that nut, if that's your fear." He rolls his eyes. "I'm actually going to change my flight. This is a dead end."

He's exaggerating about the hard-on. No way did he see that —he wouldn't stare at my junk long enough to. But we both know that I lost my distance from Tabitha in that interview.

I fucked it up.

Or maybe he doesn't know how much I fucked it up if he thinks this was a dead end. I bite back a retort that she's not a nut—hard to argue after that display, anyway—and pull out my computer as he talks to Ellie back in our office. Ignoring the pop-up for the hotel Wi-Fi, I grab a cable from my messenger bag and plug into the Ethernet port on the wall. Easier to hack into the system from within.

It doesn't take long to get into the reservations system and change our hotel room to non-refundable. Poor Ellie's gonna bear the brunt of that, but Jason's cheap and I'm not leaving Los Angeles.

Not yet.

Ms. Leyton and I need to have another talk, one without a chaperone.

Plus I need to fuck her out of my system, and since I can't actually *fuck* her, I'm going to hire the most expensive redhead call girl in the greater L.A. area and make her call me Daddy.

From the other side of the room, Jason swears. "What do you mean you can't cancel the hotel reservation?"

I glance up. "You head back if you want. I've got some work I can do here. Maybe get Ellie to pull a couple of the cold-call inquiries and I can take some client interviews over the next day or two."

He scowls, then barks the new plan into the phone.

I flip over to a new browser window and order Ellie one of those fruit basket bouquets with the chocolate strawberries. To further be a bastard, I use Jason's credit card and make the personal note sound like it's from him.

You go above and beyond. I'd be lost without you. J.

Then I buy a ticket for Tabitha's show and start looking for whatever the hell is in Fargo, North Dakota.

[10]

WILSON

THE MUSIC HALL isn't that big, maybe three thousand maximum capacity, and I was able to buy a ticket earlier this afternoon so it wasn't sold out—not like that would've stopped me—but right now it feels full. Packed to the rafters with die-hard fans who are radiating a crazy amount of energy to be able to see Tabitha Leyton sing.

She's got talent. Anyone who has watched her videos knows that. Her range is incredible, and she seeds her songs with exactly the right hooks. But before tonight, I'd have said she was just another pop star.

I was so fucking wrong.

She's standing in front of a mic stand, feet planted wide, and her hands are resting easy on her electric guitar. The last song, she played the shit out of it. This song, though, she's letting her band do the heavy lifting on the music, because she's just singing.

Just nothing. Her voice is a finely-tuned instrument and she's under my skin, a reaction that seems standard.

The lyrics soar above us, which is for the best, because they're so raw, so powerful, they'd hurt if she didn't belt them to the heavens.

From the tortured look on her face, she didn't believe they reached.

Oh, baby girl. An unfamiliar ache bursts in my chest. Does nobody else see that the pain is real for her?

There's something clawing at the back of my head. A warning—I'm aware of that much. But I can't stop myself from getting up. From finding the head of security and introducing myself, so I get invited backstage. Unlike Tabitha, he buys the badge, and my story that she's coming to the White House for a private concert and I'm doing advance reconnaissance.

Hacking pro-tip: pretend to be an insider. Works just as well with social hacking as online.

He shows me around, and tells me everything I need to know about the team around her—nobody's telling her no. She's self-destructive, powerful, and enough of a professional to keep that mostly hidden.

"Drugs?" I ask casually, like, *no biggie, but I gotta ask.*

He shakes his head. "Booze. After the show, never before. But she gets blitzed afterward."

"The reception is before the concert," I lie effortlessly.

"For the best." His radio squawks and he excuses himself to go deal with a drunk in the front of house. I make my way right to the edge of the stage. She's head-down, biting her lip as she plays her guitar. This song is about the death of a lover, and the frozen surprise of not having a chance to say goodbye.

> *Did I tell you I loved you*
> *Enough times for you to remember*
> *Won't make it to heaven, though*
> *So you're on your own there, love*
> *But you'll be fine*
> *You'll fly*

You've got wings I'll never have
You'll fly
So carry my dreams, love
And you'll be fine
You'll fly

She repeats the last line a few times until it's a whisper and she drops to her knees. The lights go black and the crowd loses its mind, cheering for her in a way I've never heard.

In the dimness, as my eyes adjust, I see she's still on her knees.

I take two steps toward her before I remember she has no idea who I am. I'm just the asshole who asked her if she'd been raped by a billionaire she hates.

Maybe she was.

Maybe she wasn't, but it came close.

It doesn't matter. A hostile witness won't do us any good, and Cole and Tag had better luck with another witness lead in New York.

I need to fly home to Washington and leave this woman behind.

As she's helped up from the polished wood of the stage, I melt into the shadows, but I don't go far.

I watch as she comes backstage, stopping less than ten feet from me. She rubs at the back of her neck, then waves her hand in the air that someone understands as a universal demand for a drink. She's handed a bottle of water, and takes a few sips before tossing it back to Handler #1.

She looks exhausted. Someone hands her a different drink, this one in a more tell-tale short glass with ice. Then another. She tosses both back like they're water.

"Do you want to shower here?" someone else asks her. A tall, willowy blonde.

Tabitha shakes her head. "Not here." Then she offers the other woman a glittery smile. "Not enough room for a crowd in the showers here, right? You coming back with me?"

The blonde laughed and nodded, her legs doing this simpering sideways wobble thing that make her look like a giraffe.

"Awesome. I need to blow off some steam. Okay." She bobs her head, then hops on the spot, recharging herself like she's got an internal battery fueled by vodka and flirting with pretty girls.

"You can do this," the blonde calls, and then she's gone.

And she does do it. Her encore is two songs, a ballad and an anthem, ending on a high note that brings down the house for a second time.

When she returns to the wings again, this time under her own steam, she peels off her tank top.

She needs to stop getting naked in front of people, an irrational part of my brain growls.

A man hands her a towel, and another shirt. She grabs his wrist. "Frankie, you coming back to my suite for the night?"

Jesus. I can't take this.

"Whatever you want, Tabitha." He gives her a smooth smile and my shoulders bunch up.

I'd like to smash his face into a million bits, but that reaction has nothing on how my body goes into overdrive when Grant approaches and slides his hand against the small of her back.

"Great show."

"Thanks." She doesn't mention her planned group activities to him. Interesting. She's invited the rest of the greater Los Angeles area.

"There are some investors—"

"I've had two drinks of—what were they, Izzie?"

"Vodquila. Best of both worlds," the blonde adds spritely,

either ignorant to the tension between the singer and her manager, or deliberately feeding the drama monster.

"Yeah." Tabitha beams at Grant. "So I'm like a loose cannon. You sure you want me to do this?"

He glowers at her. "I told you to stay sober tonight."

"Oops. I forgot."

A crash on the far side of the stage makes them all turn away from me, and I take my leave.

If she's going back to the hotel, so am I.

I pull out my phone as I make my way to my rental car and text a message to the escort service I use out here.

W: Services no longer required tonight.

[11]
TABITHA

Frankie gets my pants undone in the limo, but I don't want his hands on me tonight. We make out for a bit, then I push him aside and turn my attention to Izzie. I want to watch him fuck her.

"You want his cock, Izzie baby?"

She glances back at us over her shoulder and nods. I shove the man-child her way. He's probably twenty-three, maybe twenty-four—he's graduated college, which I haven't—but he still feels so damn young compared to what I've survived in my twenty-five years.

"Frankie, you should give the lady what she wants." I slide my hands inside my jeans and stroke my bare skin as I watch him inch down her black pants and bend her over on the wide leather seat.

The visual makes me wet, and I touch myself deeper. God, I'm sticky all over, and not in a good way. I still need to shower. He can wash my hair. Poor kid will probably love that just as much as screwing my PR girl.

He's built. Not as built as Wilson.

I close my eyes and see those grey eyes, judging me.

Ahhhh. Dude has to get out of my head. I've felt him crawling up my back and against my neck all night. If he's the reason I'm not fucking Frankie right now...

Maybe he really is a federal agent. Uptight. Repressed.

My eyelids flutter open, just enough to see the erotic tableau on the other side of the limo. Would *Wilson* rail me like that? Clothes barely undone?

I should have been more subtle this afternoon. Maybe I could have actually had sex with them instead of scaring them off.

The best part of theatre is finding out how close to the edge of reality you can slide and still be within the realm of fiction. Of telling a story and having a point, instead of just being something to gawk at.

I never fail at that. That I lost sight of that today is terrifying. I pull my hands out of my pants and reach for the vodka in the built-in bar. The limo smells like sex, and now, as I crack the seal on a top-shelf bottle I won't take a second drink from, it smells of booze, too.

My comfort zone.

And it ends too soon as we pull up in front of the Bel-Air.

Frankie and Izzie take a second to pull themselves together. My driver knows better than to open the door before I roll the window down—our signal—so when we exit the limo, Frankie in front, me in the middle, head down, and Izzie carrying my bag behind me, if there are any paparazzi, they're not going to get a very interesting shot.

Upstairs the good times continue mostly without me, and after their first round comes to a screaming conclusion—I applaud—Izzie scurries into the bathroom to get the shower going.

Yes. I need to wash off the night. And the day.

I need to wash off Wilson and his piercing gaze. His quiet

voice, and unexpected bark.

That surprised him, I could tell.

Stop thinking about him, I demand of myself. I've never been good with demands.

I pour myself another drink and stare at the phone. What was the ridiculous name he gave me? Gough. I snort and pick up the handset, immediately connecting with the concierge downstairs.

"Is Wilson Gough still here at the hotel?"

"Yes he is, ma'am."

"Don't call me that."

"My apologies, Ms. Leyton. Would you like to be connected?"

"Sure."

The phone rings a few times, then the concierge is back. "There's no answer. Would you like to leave a message?"

Not one that I want to send through a hotel employee. Or even leave on voice mail. I give the concierge a throwaway email address that I use from time to time and ask him to tell Wilson to contact me personally.

Then I down my fourth drink of the night and head to the kitchen. Smoothies by day, white toast and tequila by night. Sustenance of pop stars living on the edge.

I'm such a cliché.

I don't care. Toast is fucking awesome, and frankly, so are smoothies. Nothing without a purpose, that's my rule for whatever goes in my body. Cocks. Fingers. Food. Alcohol.

Okay, so some of them have fucked up purposes.

Whatever.

My phone vibrates on the counter.

I glance toward the bathroom. They're both in the shower now. Maybe they'll forget all about me.

Two clicks on my phone and I'm reading an email from one

Wilson *Carter*. Interesting.

From: Wilson Carter
To: TL

I was just about to let myself into your suite. This is convenient timing, are you stalking me?

I laugh, and it's such a strange sound coming from inside my body that I jump.

From: TL
To: Wilson Carter

No, that's your job. Give me ten minutes to wash off the stage sweat, then let yourself in. Or try knocking for something new and different. Bring your "partner". He's cute.

I put the phone down and shake my head, laughing again. Did I just flirt with someone who'd pretended to be a federal agent barely ten hours ago, desperate to get information from me?

I do a lot of stupid things, but I usually see them coming. Pick up the bottle and hand over the condom with the full knowledge that I'm not being totally smart.

This is different. I didn't see this coming.

Whatever happens tonight, I'm going in blind. This guy knows way more than I do.

I should be terrified.

Instead I skip to the bathroom and slid between Izzie and Frankie. Time to get the party started.

[12]

WILSON

I WASN'T KIDDING that I was about to let myself into her suite.
I'm standing in the hallway, right across from her door.

So I give her ten minutes, then I knock.

She's just wearing a robe, holding it loosely together with
one hand when she opens the door. Freshly showered, and
behind her are two more people—Frankie and Izzie from backstage. Also both in robes.

I flash my badge at them and she rolls her eyes. Okay, so she
knows it's a ruse now. I couldn't bring myself to use a fake email
address. That doesn't stop me from telling them we need the
room, because that's an effective way to be alone with her.

Izzie grabs a bag and they scurry across the hall to the other
suite.

I wait until we're alone to speak. I take the time to notice the
difference in the suite from the daytime—the only lighting is a
few lamps, and it's almost...cozy. "You summoned me?"

She scowls. "I did, but I thought I was clear in my message
that you should bring your partner."

"He's flown back to D.C."

"That's a shame." She flicks her gaze to the door, like she wants her friends to come back. Not going to happen.

"How did you know I'd stick around?"

She rolls her eyes. "You were practically gagging for an invitation into my pants. You got all turned on as an interview subject stripped down like a nut job. Someone you thought was a victim of some horrible trauma."

"You said you weren't a victim." That's weak, even to my ears. "I don't want to take advantage of you." And that's even weaker.

"Really?" She smirks.

"You're a beautiful woman..." Fuck, I suck at this. This is why I bang hookers.

She shakes her head and laughs. "That's the thing about being dirty. Sometimes it's the things we don't want to want that turn our cranks the hardest."

"That's fucked up."

"That's me." She drops her hand, letting her robe fall open. Beneath it she's naked, her bare, lush skin glowing in the lamplight. My gaze falls to the black tattoo I missed earlier, when she had her back to me, and my cock strains at my zipper as I take in what she's offering me.

Black ink swirls across her lower belly, disappearing over her hips like a reverse chastity belt—an invitation to sin.

I huff out a frustrated breath. *Fucked up? Me too.*

She moves closer, sliding her arms over my shoulders, her breath puffing hot air against my mouth. "What are you afraid of? What do you want to do to me?"

Pulling her hard against me, I grind her against my jeans, my hands gripping her hips so hard I must be leaving fingerprint shaped bruises. "Everything."

"Then let me call them back." She yanks herself out of my

grasp and paces backward, her breasts swaying hypnotically. "Because I don't do one-on-one anything."

I prowl after her. "Why?"

She shakes her head. "You don't get to ask me that. You can stay and fuck me with some friends, or you can go. We don't talk."

"We're talking right now."

She bumps into the console desk behind her and I keep going until I'm up against her. I lift her roughly, setting her ass on the desk.

Her legs wrap around me. "Go away."

"Your show tonight..."

She goes rigid in my arms. "Were you there?"

"Of course I was there."

She shoves against my chest and I step back enough to let her set her feet down. She rubs the back of her neck. "Jesus. I thought I..." She shakes her head. "Who are you? Really?"

I close my eyes. This is a bad idea. Knowing that doesn't stop me. "My name is Wilson Carter. I'm a partner in a crisis management firm in Washington, D.C."

"What is your real interest in me?"

At the moment, it's fucking her silly, but since we've gotten real for a second, that's on the back burner. "That we didn't lie about. We're investigating Gerome Lively."

She stiffens. "I really don't have anything to do with him."

"Does your manager?"

Her face pales. "How good are you at your job?"

"The best."

"Then I'm sure you'll figure that out soon enough on your own." She sticks me with a cold look and leans back against the console. The ivory silk of her robe is a luxurious frame for the perfection of her body. Heavy breasts. Dark pink nipples. Enough curve to her belly to be interesting, but she's all muscle.

And then there are those wings across the lowest curve, framing her bare pussy. I drop to my knees and press a kiss there, on the ink, and she tangles her fingers in my hair, urging me lower.

I'll get there soon enough. I'll make her scream, because I want to consume her. I want to devour her taste until her scent is permanently imprinted on my skin. But right now I'm more interested in the tattoo. I trace my fingers over the edge of it, using two hands. When she squirms, I shift one hand to squeeze her hip. Hold her in place.

Lighter now, I brush over each wing with my fingers.

It's when my touch slides from one wing to another, over the scrolling heart in the middle, then I feel the faint ridge of scar tissue.

She freezes.

Has nobody else ever touched her like this? Obviously she's free with her body.

Not so much with the tattoo?

It's an old scar, and the tattoo ink fully disguises it to the eye.

A horizontal cut, a few inches wide and right at her pubic bone.

I press my forehead against her belly.

You've got wings I'll never have
You'll fly
So carry my dreams, love
And you'll be fine

Tabitha Leyton doesn't have children.

But she gave birth to one, and not recently.

I rise to my feet. Barefoot, she's tiny, and in order to kiss her I need to bend over.

Picking her up is a hell of a lot easier. Her waist is nothing in my hands, and she gasps as I hoist her up high, easily holding her against me as I take her mouth.

Frustrated anger pours through me and into her as the kiss goes from zero to sixty in the blink of an eye. Her lips part and her tongue darts out. It's an invitation I'll always accept, I know that in my gut.

This woman—messed up, hostile, tragic—owns my soul somehow. She can take anything she wants from me. And even if she doesn't ask for anything, I still give it.

I've never been a caregiver. I'm not sure I know how, not in a healthy way. But as our mouths move together, as I stroke my tongue against her and swallow her protests and her fears, as I hold her tight and let her haul me closer...I can give her this.

I can say, *I see you, baby girl. I don't know who you are or what the hell happened to you, but I see your darkest secret and I still want you.*

Not with actual words, of course.

We're going to pretend now.

We're going to hide from the truth.

But we're going to do it together.

[13]

WILSON

I SETTLE her more firmly on the table and spread her legs wide. I'm still dressed in my jeans and dress shirt. I rolled up my sleeves when I was waiting for her earlier, but she's gloriously naked and I want—no, need—to be buried to the hilt inside her, so my clothes are a problem. I roughly undo the buttons on my shirt as she watches me.

I'd have gotten it all the way off, too, if she hadn't reached between her legs and touched herself.

I can't explain the hold this woman has on me. Fuck it, I don't want to explain it. If I think too long about that, too hard, I'll stop myself before we get to the finish line.

I grab her wrist with a growl and pull her hands to my chest, then my lips, where I suck the taste of her arousal off her skin. *Mine.*

"Bed," she whispers, scratching her short nails into my hair as she wraps her arms around me. The light touch sends a bolt of desire straight to my balls.

"No," I growl. "I want you right here, right now."

"Someone might come in."

"Then they'll have to watch." This is important. I glare at

her. "I'm not sharing you. *Just you and me.* No fucking orgies to hide behind. But I don't care who sees me take you, you got that? Nothing you can say or do will shock me. I'm not...Fuck, Tabitha. I'm not a possessive man. But when it comes to you, I think I am, and you're just going to have to deal with that."

"You don't want to see me lick someone's sweet pussy while you pound into me?"

That's hot, I can't deny it. And I'm an asshole for not taking what she's offering—for demanding something most definitely *not* on offer.

"You like the taste of pussy?" I slide my middle finger along her slit, easily finding her soaking wet entrance. I circle her slick skin as she clenches helplessly, coating my finger with her juices before lifting my hand to her mouth. "Then suck."

She does, greedily, but it's not the taste of herself that she's hungry for. She sucks my entire finger deep into her hot, wet mouth, her tongue pulling my digit nearly into her throat.

The vacuum seal makes my dick surge against the fly of my jeans.

"Get my cock out," I tell her roughly. Her eyes go wide and I press my finger hard against her tongue. I'm not fucking joking. She's got me halfway to coming, and it's not going to be in my pants.

It's going to be down her million-dollar throat.

And then I'm going to get hard again—if I even go soft at all —and my next load will be in her off-limits pussy.

Nothing about Tabitha is off-limits to me.

Not anymore.

Her hands are like magic, getting my fly down and my cock out in a flash. She makes this hungry little sound that kills me as she gives me a preliminary squeeze and a drop of pre-come appears for her.

"Lick it up," I order, and she scrambles to her knees, tongue out, eyes closed. I cover her hand with my own, rubbing the fat head of my dick against her tongue, then I butt it right up against her lips. "Open. Ahhh. Yes. Good. Girl. Fuck. Yeah. Swallow."

I pet her cheek as she pulls me deep, doing exactly what she promised on my finger. God, she's good. My eyes drift shut and I snap them open again. I'm not going to miss a second of this. She's incredible. Her dark hair flows over her bare shoulders, creamy pale skin swaying back and forth as she puts her entire body into sucking me dry. Her tits sway between us, and I picture stretching her out on a bed. They're big enough they'd still be fuckable when she's on her back.

I need them in my mouth.

I need my dick buried deep in her pussy.

With a growl I slide my thumb along the corner of her mouth, getting her attention. "Enough."

She whimpers as I lean down and pick her up, carrying her to the couch.

I set her down and return to my knees, kissing her thighs and then burying my face in her pussy as I rid myself of my shirt.

My first impression of her, when I started digging, was that she was pure sex and sin. Then we met in person and I saw her fear. On stage, she's something else. Larger than life and transcendent.

Now she's warm and real.

Sexy, yes, but there's nothing sinful about the way she wraps her thighs around my head. Soft and eager. She tastes like unbridled desire. No games, no rules, no contract or texted instructions.

I touch her again as I work her clit with my tongue. Circle, circle, flick. My fingers tease her entrance, then slide in when she bucks her hips.

Begging for it. Greedy girl. Good girl.

She grips me tight and my dick throbs, ready for the condom I brought with me.

But first I need to know what she tastes like when she flies free.

I want to give her the wings she thinks she'll never have. I want to show her she's an angel on Earth. My heart is pounding as I stroke my fingers in and out of her clenching cunt, curving up to find that spot that makes her gasp.

That makes her moan.

I rub her there, as I suck her clit, and as she tenses beneath me, I exhale, hot breath against her sex as I fuck a third finger into her, stretching her wider than she expected.

Her hips jerk off the couch, her legs splaying wide, and I follow her, pulling her clit into my mouth one last time as she curls up around my head and holds on tight.

I grin to myself against the inside of her thigh.

Beautiful.

[14]

TABITHA

I MAY HAVE BLACKED out there for a second. Not sure. Wilson's moving me now, like I'm a rag doll. He settles on the couch, holding me on his lap. He's naked.

No, not fully, I realize as I shift back to regular consciousness. His jeans are shoved down to his knees. I can feel them behind me.

But from thighs up, we're naked together, and between our bodies, his cock rises. Thick and hard. Curved nicely, and there's more of that delicious pre-come forming on the tip.

I make another hopeless sound as he covers it up with a condom, but then his hands are on my hips, and he's urging me up and onto him.

Oh my God.

I feel like a teenager again.

Maybe that's because the last time—

No. Not going there.

But yeah. This...I don't do this.

"I don't either," he mutters, and I bite my lip.

What else did I say out loud?

He holds me above him, just circling the tip inside my pussy lips. I'm so sloppy for him he could probably just slide in—I'm sure of it. Until he actually starts to slide in, and I have to take a deep breath, because *holy shit.*

I mean, I've had him in my mouth. I know he's big.

But there's nothing quite like *this*. His gaze glued to mine. His hands, branding my hips with a bruising hold as he rocks into me. Up. Up. Up.

Each pulse pressing inexorably deeper.

Tearing my heart in two.

"Wilson," I breath.

"Right here with you," he grinds out.

I wrap my arms around him, giving in to my need to touch him, to taste him. I kiss his mouth, his jaw, his neck...he tastes like a fearless spring wind, salty and warm, but there's a coolness, too.

Like he really doesn't do this. Like he's used to this being mechanical.

Dirty.

I know all about that.

He palms my ass, one cheek in each hand, and I press back against his touch. Encouraging him.

He touches me there, stroking everywhere, and I roll my hips. Back into his touch. Forward and down onto his cock. Faster. Harder.

As I rise on my knees to get more leverage, he nuzzles my chest, and I cup my breasts for him. I offer myself to him, and he looks at me first.

We hold that for a moment, another pause before more dirty.

And oh, then it gets *so* dirty. He sucks my nipples deep, first one, then the other, and once he pulls them to aching, puffy peaks with his mouth, he pinches them hard.

I swallow my moan, but he slaps my ass and tells me he

wants to hear it. "Don't deny me those sounds," he growls, and I can't. I scream his name as he drives his cock into me, ruthlessly now, holding me in place as he strokes in and out. His pace is whipping me towards a second orgasm so fast I don't know what to do. I'm a vessel for him to come inside, to hold and plunder and fuck and consume.

I'm lit up in technicolor wonder. Outside my body, I can feel him, hear him, and taste him as I sink my teeth into his delicious shoulder, but beyond the points where we're touching, nothing else exists.

It's just me and Wilson, and he's playing the most beautiful music with my body. His lips return to my breasts, licking and sucking there as I crest the highest wave I've ever ridden, then his mouth crashes into mine as he joins me in a stuttering, explosive finale.

It takes us a lot longer than a minute to disentangle this time.

I flop over, and he gets rid of the condom, then joins me.

We kiss and touch for longer than I'd ever expect—again, am I acting like the teenage girl who never got to neck in her parents' basement? Am I reverse-rounding the bases?

And why does this still feel so damn *good*? The sex is over. I should be in a scalding shower right now, scrubbing my skin and waiting for the melatonin to kick in so I can pass out.

But I don't want to pass out. I never want this night to end.

He's playing with my hair when I finally get up the nerve to ask him about something he said during sex. "What did you mean, you don't do this either?"

He leans over and picks up his shirt, helping me into it. He takes his time before answering, filling the silence with a very thorough worship of my breasts again. When I keep looking at him in amusement—because he's clever, but so am I—he sighs. "That's maybe a conversation best left for another time."

"Why?"

"Because I want to fuck you again, and if I admit that I only ever pay for it, you're not going to let me." He glances up at me from beneath the dirty blond flop of hair that I find so irresistible, and I laugh.

"Really?"

"Shut up, I'm being honest."

"Hookers?"

"Call girls."

"Gross." But I say it without any heat, because I secretly like that he doesn't date. I mean, it's gotta be expensive, but so is hiring staff that will fuck me, so I can't judge. I pick up his hand and press it to my chest. "All the time?"

He shrugs, then nods. "Not frequently, either."

That is a shame for vaginas everywhere, except again, I secretly like it. His beautiful cock is all mine.

Or was. For tonight.

Reality slams back into me and I roll off his lap, holding his shirt closed around me.

"You look good in my shirt," he whispers once he catches me in the bedroom. He gently pushes me onto my back.

I grin up at him. "You look good without it."

"Perfect."

We fall asleep at some point, after making out and using another condom in the shower. When I wake up, I pull his shirt back on and pad out to the kitchen to get a smoothie. No clue what Wilson's going to have for breakfast, but maybe he likes kale.

If not, I can make him toast.

It's as close as I'll ever get to a domestic scene, so I'm going to cling to it as long as possible.

"Took you long enough to wake up," Grant drawls from the couch and I scream, dropping my smoothie as I whirl around.

"What are you doing in here?"

"Good morning." He gives me a cold look that says he knows I spent the night with someone.

There's no point pretending that's not an exceptional event.

"You need to leave."

I'd opened my mouth to say it, but it wasn't my voice. From behind me, Wilson's voice vibrates with authority and he steps forward, blocking me from Grant's view.

Oh, shit.

I can't see Grant anymore, but I don't need to. He probably gives Wilson an amused look here. "I do?"

"Tabitha will call you when she's not busy." I wince at the heroics. That's not going to land well. Not that Wilson can't take Grant—I had a repeated tour of his body last night. I know just how muscled he his, the power he hides on that apparently lean frame.

Nothing lean about him once you strip off the clothes.

And since I'm still wearing his shirt...

Grant would be an idiot to mess with Wilson.

That's the problem. He's always been an idiot, ever since he flashed a smile and a business card at me and got more than he ever bargained in return.

Or maybe he's not an idiot. Maybe this is his revenge, a decade in the making. Because the first time I allow myself to feel happiness since the night I lost Keegan, Grant's here to take it away.

I know what he's going to say. I lift my hand to touch Wilson's back, to somehow hold on to the connection that Grant's about to blow to smithereens.

"You think I'm the one who's going to leave here?" Grant snorts and I try to say something, but my voice doesn't work. I'm already retreating inside the broken shell I call Tabitha Leyton.

"Look man, I don't know who you think you are, but there's

a thing called common human decency, and right now you're not really exhibiting it."

"You don't know who I am?"

Wilson sighs.

My heart breaks.

Grant wins the day with the hollowest of victories. "I'm her husband."

I can feel Tabitha behind me, shaking like a leaf. I want to turn to her, but I can't give this guy my back.

And I need a minute before I look her in the face and see that it's true.

Because I know it is. All the pieces slide together.

She doesn't have much of an identity because Tabitha is an *assumed* identity. Which means she's also someone else, and as that someone else, she had a baby and married this man, for reasons that might be connected, but the key is that *I don't know them.*

I'm nobody to her.

I've bought into yet another layer of lies.

Grant smirks at me.

I'm not giving him the satisfaction of a response.

"Hope you wrapped it up, anyway," he tosses off as he walks to the first bedroom like he owns the place. "She'll let anything stick it in her."

I'm across the room before he puts his hand on the door. I slam into him, shoulder first, and the crunch isn't nearly satisfying enough as we tumble into the bedroom and spin around. I slam my fist into his guts twice as I back him up against the wall inside the door, two quick shots that'll make him pee blood, then I get my forearm under his chin and I press.

Hard.

"I'm your new worst enemy," I whisper, spitting in his face as I do. I'm shaking with white-hot rage, the likes of which I haven't felt in years, and if he moves, I will kill him.

He freezes.

"You think a casual insult scares me off? You think I'm under any delusions about not being used by *your wife?*" I nudge his legs apart with my knee, lifting him higher up on the wall so his toes just dance helplessly above the ground. He knows what's coming, and I make him wait for it.

It's only when doubt starts to swirl in his eyes—maybe I won't do it?—that I jerk my knee up, driving his balls hard into his body.

More blood to piss out.

Asshole.

I step back and let him crumple to the floor, then I back out of the room, closing the door behind me.

There's still the small matter of *Tabitha* to deal with. She's staring at me, eyes wide, mouth covered with her pale little fingers.

"Don't—" I stop and shake my head. "You have nothing to fear from me."

"I'm not..." She gives me an incredulous look. "I'm not *afraid* of you, Wilson. But why did you do that?"

"He said—"

"You think that's the first time he's called me a slut?" She laughs hysterically. "That's a regular good morning around here."

"That fucking shit doesn't fly with me."

She gives me a look of disbelief. "So?"

"I'm not going to let him talk about you like that."

"You don't get a say in it. *We* are not a thing. You need to leave."

My jaw clenches so hard I think I may have fractured something. I don't fucking care. "We aren't done."

"He wasn't lying. It's a secret, for kind of stupid reasons, but it's true. We're married." Her chest rises and falls in sharp, stuttering jerks. She thinks that's enough to push me away?

I prowl towards her, and her eyes widen. Pleading...for what? To tell her it's going to be okay? That I'll keep her secret?

I will.

But I'm not letting her go.

Because I know the truth. I stop a foot from her—close enough to pull her into my arms.

I don't.

Close enough to share her breath and see the pain in her eyes. I look at her long and hard, letting her see that I see her. "*Why* are you married?"

"That's none of your business."

"Your pussy wrapped around my cock says otherwise."

"You have a very old-fashioned way of looking at fucking, then."

"Never did until last night."

"That's too bad."

"For your husband. Not for you, and not for me." I flick my gaze to the door and the asshole on the other side. I need to remember that whatever fucked up situation Tabitha is in, she was in it before I stormed into her world. And she's a grown-up. Sort of. "Are you safe with him?"

She laughs. "Yes."

"I can't leave you with him."

She shakes her head. "You need to. I'm going to call a doctor for him. And I'm never truly alone with him. You need to go home. This isn't a fairy tale, Wilson."

"You think that's what I want?"

"I think...neither of us expected this. Right?" She shifts closer and presses her hand against my cheek. I'm seething, and her touch doesn't cool my rage. She's fearless in the face of it, though. "So we need to pretend last night was a dream."

How she locks everything up. A dream. A song. Words on the page, scratched over and over again until the letters turn to music notes. Am I going to recognize myself in a song on her next album?

I shake my head. "This isn't over. I'll see you again soon, Tabitha."

She gives me the longest, saddest look, then looks away. And when she looks back, she's armed with razor blades instead of words. "Think I'll be fucking someone else when you do?"

My nostrils flare. That's not going to work. "Think you'll fuck anyone else alone between now and then?" I lean in and ghost my lips against hers. "If you do, you let me know. Then we can be done."

I want to imagine I see a tear in her eye as I step back. That it's not glossy fierceness, but actual feelings that I've stirred inside her.

I want to know she's half as affected by me as I am by her.

I'll be left hanging on that point forever, because she turns her back on me, not waiting to see me out.

I stand in the empty living room of a suite in the Bel-Air. Less than a day has passed since I first stormed into this room, not knowing what I'd find.

Now I've lost my shirt, my heart, and my sanity, all in one fell swoop.

Because my only thought as I stare at the closed door, on the other side of which is my lover and her *husband*, is...

Mine.

Dirty Love

part three

dirty secrets

[16]

TABITHA

I SPEND the next three days in the studio. They pass in a blur.

Wilson has altered me on a primal level. I haven't even wanted to drink, and that's not a good thing. It's also definitely a temporary thing—I'm not giving his dick or his dirty mouth any credit for reforming my bad girl ways.

I like my bad girl ways.

Fuck him.

Fuck him for changing me, for leaving me, for listening to me.

Grant has decided to pretend nothing happened, but only on the most superficial level. He's pissed at me, and it comes across in how he snipes about the songs, my voice, the tracks we're laying down.

He doesn't like any of it, because he doesn't like me.

As I often do when he's mad at me and I hate everything about my life, I fantasize about leaving.

A tell-all interview. Discovered on the streets of Seattle. A seduction—into the music world, into Grant's bed.

A pregnancy.

Panic.

Drugs.

And that's where any possible path to freedom freezes. I can't. I just—

"Tabitha, that sounded great. Let's do it one more time, from the top." From the other side of the glass, the producer gives me a thumbs up that means the complete opposite. That take was terrible, we still don't have it.

The words stick in my throat, and when I miss my cue, he pauses the music. "You want a minute?"

I close my eyes. No, I'm not fucking weak. With a rough, hard shake of my head, I gesture for him to start again.

Some of my songs I write myself. This one is co-written and a bit over produced. I don't love the first few lines, they're kind of cliched. It's supposed to be...an accessible kind of edgy, they say. Edgy shouldn't be accessible, but I lost that battle. So far today I've been trying to hit them with a pop enthusiasm I'm just not feeling.

This time, I ignore what we've talked about and I ease into the song, my voice soft on the first two lines. Tentative. Like I don't know if this is a good idea.

It's not, really.

And suddenly I'm fifteen again. Being offered something to help me chill out, then something to amp me up.

Take a chance on a wicked line
Slick smile, knowing eyes
You'd talk me into heaven
Easy trick, tricky trespass

Tumble
Stumble
Get back up
Turn and smile

That was nothing
And you never miss a beat

Take a chance on a wicked line
Slick smile, knowing eyes
You'll be my dirty secret
Undoing, done just right

My voice grows stronger as I sing, turns seductive. By the time I'm telling my corrupter that he'll be my dirty secret, I know what's going on. And I like it.

Fuck. I don't want any twelve-year-olds singing along to this. My voice cracks on the next refrain, and the producer waves me off.

Instead of starting again, he gets up and waves me into the other room.

I don't need a pep talk.

I need a do-over on the entire year when I was fifteen.

When I push through the insulated door, I don't stop. "I'll be back in a few. Just—give me a few." And I keep going.

I'm shaking from head to toe by the time I get to the room across the hall where my stuff is stashed. I close the door behind me and slump against it. Every muscle in my body aches and my head throbs. I can't keep doing this, but I have to.

On the other side of the room, from inside my purse, my phone rings.

Rings.

I never leave the ringer on, it's always on vibrate.

I scowl. Did someone fuck with my stuff while I was in the studio?

It rings again.

I scramble across the room and pull it out. The screen is

blinking, which is weird, and if this were any other time in my life, I'd have turned it off and walked away. Thrown it out.

But three days ago, my life was turned upside down by the kind of man who could probably reach inside my phone and make it ring.

I tap the answer button and hold it up to my ear.

I don't say anything.

He does, though. "What's wrong?"

"Who is this?" My heart pounds against my ribs. I know exactly who it is. I grip the phone tighter against my ear. "How did—"

"Tell me what's wrong, Tabitha." Wilson's voice is hard, strained.

I turn in a slow circle. "Where are you?"

"At the hotel."

"I told you leave me alone."

"And I did."

"I told you to leave!" My voice rises hysterically, but I'm not sure I did. "Why are you still in L.A.?"

He doesn't answer that question. "Do I need to come and get you?"

"You can't do this."

"We need to talk about that."

"We can't."

"I'll find a way." He takes a deep breath, then slows himself down. "You freaked out in there."

"How do you—" I press my fist against my mouth to stop from asking the rest of that question. Oh God, I don't want to know the answer.

He tells me anyway. "You've been going to the same studio for three days. I'm monitoring it now."

"And my phone?"

"The ringer can be turned on remotely. There's a lot I can do from a distance, Tabitha. Including protecting you."

"I don't need your protection."

"And I can be someone who knows you're upset, and ask you what's wrong."

"I don't need that, either."

"Maybe I do."

"I find that hard to believe." I laugh, because what the fuck has happened to me? "Who are you?"

"I'm yours."

"That's insane."

"Yeah." He laughs, too, but not as maniacally as I do. "Look, you're okay? I'll let you go if you are."

"I'm..." Not okay. "I'm singing a song I don't want to sing."

"Then don't."

"Oh, that's a complicated impossible option."

"I won't ask why, but I'm curious."

"I won't tell you, so stifle that." I sigh. "I'm fine now. I just needed a minute to get my shit together."

"Sing a different song," he says softly. "Or go and sing the hell out of that one. I thought it sounded great, for what it's worth."

"It's..."

"Is it real? Is it your story?"

I swallow hard. "Sort of. But I didn't write most of it. So it's...uncomfortable, you know? Like people might see that it's real."

"You don't shy away from those types of songs."

"I write them differently."

He lets my words just hang between us. He doesn't say anything. He doesn't need to.

I write them differently. "I gotta go."

"Kill it," he says. Then he hangs up.

And I do.

I totally kill it.

I head back into the producer's bay, prop my hands on my hips, and declare, "The words are all wrong."

———

It takes another six hours, but we re-write the song and it fucking rocks. I'm so amped by the time we finish that when Grant throws his arm around my shoulders and says we need to celebrate—the first thing he's said to me in days—I manage not to push him away.

I do want to celebrate. I pivot into Frankie's arms, then twirl Izzie around in a circle before laying a wet kiss on the cheek of my new back-up singer, Ginger.

"Back to your hotel?" she asks, her eyes twinkling.

I'm tempted, but the motivation for saying yes would be all wrong. "I'm hungry, actually."

We call for two cars, and when they arrive, I drag Izzie and Ginger into the first one, leaving Grant to ride with Frankie and the producer.

We head to a tapas bar in West Hollywood that's more club than restaurant. Before long the table we're standing at is littered with plates and glasses, and I'm three shots into celebrating in style. I don't hear my phone ring at first, because the music is loud, but Ginger's next to me and she points to my bag.

I pull it out, ignoring Grant's curious look. It's a text, not a call, and again the screen is flashing. The phone number isn't legit, but I know who it's from anyway.

003-3000: having a good time?

Tabitha: not now, have a stalker

I add a winking emoticon to soften the words, then reach for my drink, pretending my pulse isn't racing as I wait for his response. When it comes, I immediately silence the ringer, but I don't look at the screen. I wait until Grant gets dragged into a conversation with an industry person that stops by, then check it out.

003-3000: just watching your back

Tabitha: not necessary

003-3000: I'll be the judge of that

That shouldn't turn me on. Liquid heat rushes though me, a mad wildfire.

Tabitha: we need to have a talk about boundaries

003-3000: we can talk whenever you want

Tabitha: not now, I'm celebrating

003-3000: I can tell; I want you to have fun

Tabitha: are you sure about that?

003-3000: definitely...ask your friend to dance

I glance at Ginger, then look around the room. Where is he? It's crowded tonight, and there are too many shadows.

Maybe I'll take his suggestion after all. I click out of the text message screen and my phone stops flickering. When I click back into my messages, there's no trace of that conversation.

Who the hell are you, Wilson Carter?

A question for another time. I put my phone away in my bag, hand it to Frankie to keep an eye on, and grab Ginger's hand. "Come on, let's dance."

[17]

TABITHA

WE DANCE FOR A COUPLE HOURS. There aren't any more text messages, and I never see him, but when everyone else decides to go to an all-night club on Sunset Boulevard, I beg off and head back to the hotel.

I hate being alone, but I don't think there's much risk of that when I get upstairs.

I'm not wrong. The elevator stops on the third floor, and my pulse jacks up as the doors open.

Wilson gets on. His jaw is hard, his eyes piercing. He doesn't say anything, but he presses the sixth floor button. As he moves, I catch the scent of him, cool spring morning and fearlessness. It's the height of summer in Los Angeles, but that doesn't touch him. And beneath that sweet, grassy scent is something more masculine. Something familiar.

His scent carries with it markers of our night together. Reminders of a bond I didn't ask for and don't know how to handle, but one that made me happy, too.

For better or worse, I'm glad to see him. No, glad isn't it. Glad doesn't touch how I feel.

Relief, hunger, ache...

I'm his.

There's no denying it as he stands next to me.

When the doors open again, we both get off.

His room is right across from the stairwell. He lets me in, and my skin tingles as I move past him, but he doesn't touch me.

He still doesn't say anything.

It's a small room, standard size. A bed, a television on a dresser, and a small desk. That's covered in computer gear. A laptop, a tablet, a few black and silver bricks that look like external hard drives. Wires running everywhere.

My pulse leaps, a nervous beat I can feel in my neck.

"This is dangerous," I whisper.

He crowds behind me, his hands on my hips. Rough, demanding. "Wouldn't want it any other way."

Lord help me, but that works. It makes me wet, it makes me ache. "I..." Tipping my head back against his chest, I close my eyes.

"I know you're tired," he whispers. "Let me take care of you."

"I'm not yours," I protest weakly.

"Shut up."

"You aren't listening to me."

"I am. I'm just disregarding your protest. Maybe I am not yours yet, but you are definitely mine. Mine to protect and mine to worry about."

"How can you know that? We just met."

"Life has a fucking twisted sense of humor. I promise you that five days ago I thought I would never have someone like you in my life." He makes a disbelieving sound. "And then you... were you."

I don't know what to do with that kind of tenderness. And when I spin around in his arms, from the look on his face, neither does he.

When we crash together, there's nothing tender about it. He hauls me up his body as he consumes my mouth. I kiss him back, desperate for more. Biting, tasting, soul-stealing and everything in between. I want to climb inside him, be his and let the rest of the world go. Never stop kissing him.

I want so much that I can't have.

With a groan, he squeezes me to him and turns. But instead of the bed, he carries me into the bathroom, bumping into the door on the way in. He sets me on the counter and leans in, kissing me softly this time. So soft it hurts, and I push him away.

His eyes pierce into me, seeing my resistance, my fear. He cups my cheek and holds my face in front of his, but he doesn't kiss me again.

And then after a long, agonizing beat, he steps back and I slide off the counter.

The bathroom's small and cramped with us both in here. I catch a glimpse of us in the mirror as I turn. He looks almost preppy compared to my bad girl get up. Black skinny jeans. Grey tank top over a black bra. Silver necklace, dark lipstick, heavy eye makeup. And he towers over me, a blond-haired and blue-eyed avenging angel. Blue jeans and a dress shirt rolled up to his elbows.

Unspoken angst hangs heavy, but apparently we're going to ignore that. He pats my hip. "Get naked. I want to wash the night off you."

"Shower sex? Hell yes."

He laughs. "I'm going to give you a bath."

Oh. That sends a weird thrill through my belly. Okay.

I take off my jewelry and tank top as he turns the taps to start the flow of hot water. He frowns at the tiny hotel toiletry bottles on the counter, then grabs the body wash and empties it into the tub.

I've just sat down on the toilet to take off my sandals when he turns back and kneels in front of me.

Wordlessly, he undoes the strap at my ankle. Then he takes the other foot and braces it against his thigh, releasing me from that sandal, too.

"Up."

I stand, and he unbuttons my jeans. His fingers graze my tattoo and I shiver. The trembling gets stronger as he leans in and kisses my belly.

"Shhh..." He works my jeans down my legs, his palms skimming my flesh and raising goosebumps everywhere he touches.

The tub is almost full now. He turns me around, facing it, and takes off my bra, leaving me naked and ready to be cleaned.

"Hair up?"

I shake my head. It's not what I'd usually use, but the hotel conditioner will be fine, and I want to wash the day off every inch of my body.

"In you get." He holds my hand until I'm stretched out beneath the bubbles.

I take a deep breath, then slide under the water, getting my hair wet. I use my fingers to scrub my scalp before I surface, an when I do, Wilson's still crouched beside the tub.

A half-smile transforms his face. "Feel good?"

"Yeah."

"Can I wash your hair?"

I don't use regular shampoo—I pay way too much for my hair to look this good to risk it to the crap they normally put in that stuff—but hotel conditioner is fine, and I tell him just to use that. I add a pleased little smile at the end so he knows I'm appreciative.

He stands up easily and twists to grab the conditioner bottle. He's a big guy, and seems bigger still when he's fully dressed and I'm naked in the tub.

The fatigue that had hung over me when I arrived is gone now. Heat blooms inside me as I greedily look at his legs, the tight curve of his ass, his narrow hips. I've done a lot of kinky shit in my time, but nobody has ever given me a bath before.

It's almost cute, but I don't do cute.

So when he turns around, I'm waiting for him, kneeling in the tub, my legs spread wide, everything from my hips up displayed for him above the water.

I'm at exactly the right level to see his erection swell behind the fly of his jeans. I take my time dragging my attention up to his face, and when I get there, his gaze is hot.

Scalding, really.

"This can only be tonight," I say.

We both know he doesn't accept that. But he bites his lower lip and rakes his gaze over my body. "Then I better make it good enough for you change your mind."

That's where he's wrong. I gave up my right to choose my own path a long time ago. But I'm not selfless. If he's game to fuck me silly, I'm not going to push him away until he's done. "Do your worst."

[18]

WILSON

Fucking temptress.

My jeans are uncomfortably tight as I loom over Tabitha's naked, bubble-slicked body. My worst? "Can you handle that?"

"I can handle anything," she says, her nipples tightening as she looks up at me. "Do what you want with me. I'm yours to play with."

"Until you bite." I grin and grab a towel to kneel on. "Turn around. I'm going to wash your hair." I wait until she's settled with her back to me, then I gather her wet strands in my fist and tug her backward so my mouth is next to her ear. "Get you squeaky clean everywhere."

"Promise or a threat?" She twists her head as much as she can and water runs down my arm, soaking into my rolled-up sleeve.

"Both." I release her and squeeze conditioner into my palm. I carefully work it into her thick red hair, coating the strands before massaging her scalp with my fingers.

"You're good at this," she whispers.

"First time." I clear my throat, trying not to think about how good it feels to hold her head in my hands. How I could turn her around and get her to blow me. A quick screw isn't going to bind her to me any more than the other night did.

I need to get under her skin. Fucking is a means to an end tonight.

But she's just as equally interested in getting under my skin. I soap up her back, then her sides, edging onto the swell of her breasts, then down to her waist, and the whole time, she's talking smack to me.

And it's making my dick harder than I thought possible.

"I didn't take you for the guardian type," she breathes.

"Is that how you think I see you? Someone to take care of?"

"Isn't it?" She shifts, lifting the curve of her bottom out of the water. A red flag invitation to be violated there. I reach for the conditioner. "Do you see me as a girl in distress, needing rescue?"

"Is that what you want? A father figure to protect you, baby girl?"

She freezes.

Maybe I've gone too far. Maybe my dick is genuinely cutting off the blood flow to my brain.

"I can take care of myself," she says softly. "And I've had enough father figures ruin my life, thank you very much."

But she follows that with a slow, inviting glance at me over her shoulders.

I raise one eyebrow. "Should I finish what I started?"

She nods, and I coat my fingers with conditioner.

"Are you mine to play with?"

"Yes."

I stroke my index finger over the curve of her ass. "Good. Hold still."

[19]

TABITHA

THERE'S nothing quite like being ordered not to move. My senses go on high alert and my eyelids flutter shut as he skims his fingertips between my ass cheeks and over my sensitive flesh there, then lower, leaving a slippery trail from one hole to the next.

"So smooth, Miss Leyton. That's fucking sexy as hell." He circles my clit, making me bloom, making me want more, before sliding back again.

He's totally going to finger my ass, the teasing jerk.

I tilt my hips. *Do it*, I urge him with my body language.

But he just touches me lightly, circling my clenched hole. Not pressing inside.

"I don't like to be teased," I mutter.

"Then it's too bad you told me I could do whatever I wanted, isn't it?" He drops his hand into the warm water, splashing it against the inside of my thighs.

His next touch is against my pussy again, a finger dipping inside me, then dragging my wetness over my folds.

He turns his hand so his thumb can press into me from behind, and still I hold steady.

Again, this isn't how I have sex.

I'm restless to move, to fuck back against his hand. To get my self off, to use him.

Taking what he wants to give me and nothing more is foreign. Uncomfortable. Hot, though.

Definitely hot.

The restlessness moves inside me, pushing at the inside of skin. It cues a sharp awareness of his touch, my reaction. The feel of his hand and the sounds we're both making.

My sighs and his groans as he sinks further into me, stretching me out.

"You like that."

I do. "You like it, too."

"I love it." He stretches his fingers inside my pussy. "Hot little cunt." His thumb flexes, too. "Tight little ass."

"Ah, yes..." I give in and roll my hips, but his other hand shoots out, his forearm wrapping around me as he pulls me back against him.

"Naughty girl."

"Punish me?"

"Not a punishment if you're begging for it." He eases his fingers out of me. "I think you're clean enough, now." He presses his face into my neck, and this close, I can tell his breaths aren't as controlled as I thought they were. "Time to rinse off."

Wilson doesn't pull the shower curtain closed. Instead, he leans back against the counter and watches me from behind hooded eyelids, his fists white-knuckled in the towel he's holding.

The second I turn off the water, he's picking me up. Fluffy cotton and strong arms surround me as he carries me back to the bed.

"At some point we're going to need to discuss the fact that

my legs do in fact work," I say over a bubbly laugh that sounds nothing like me.

"Hmm. Do they?" He dumps me out of his arms and I bounce on the mattress. "Let me check."

He picks up one of my feet and rests it against his dress shirt. Naked girl, fully-dressed man. It's dirty and wrong. I love it. I wiggle my toes as he dries my leg with the towel. I leave wet toe-prints on his shirt as I walk my foot down his perfect torso.

"You work out."

"Nix does." He picks up my other leg and casually pushes the first one down and out, making me spread myself for him.

"Who is Nix?"

"A street fighter."

"Okay... Are you talking about yourself in the third person?"

He grins. "Yeah. Show Nix your pussy."

That he's being weird is hardly a reason not to comply with a perfect delicious request. I reach between my legs and run my fingertips over my sex, parting the lips to show him how wet I am.

I'm shameless. I'm a slut. This is nothing.

He works his way up my thigh, drying me off all the way until our fingers brush. And then he keeps going, making me groan, because I want his touch, not my own. He rolls me over and dries my back, my hair. His solid thighs, still clad in denim, rub rough against my skin when he straddles my legs.

When he finally tosses the towel aside, he doesn't turn me again.

Instead he jerks my hips into the air, so I need to scramble to get my legs under me, and spanks my ass lazily. "Good girl."

"Try harder."

"Bad girl?"

"Closer."

He laughs and leans over me, brushing his lips against my

shoulder blade. "Baby girl. I remember." He curls his hand around my biceps. "I remember everything. And it's not enough. I want to find out more about what makes you tick, my little Tabitha. My secret girl."

Oh. My chest heats up. "Yes."

"Yes?"

I press my hips into the air, suddenly needy for him to touch me. "Please."

He bites me next, pulling the flesh of my back up and into his mouth. A gentle tug, but the reminder of his intent—to claim and possess me—is clear.

The ache between my legs intensifies.

He works down my spine, kissing and licking and marking me until my thighs are wet from how much I want him. When he gets to my ass, he grips my hips, spreading me open.

"Are you sensitive here?" he asks, his breath hot against my skin.

"Yes."

He growls.

"Was I supposed to say, 'I don't know, Mister, nobody has never touched me there before.'?"

"Always." He nips at my butt cheek.

I close my eyes as he slowly laves his tongue down my crease. "Ahhhh. Nobody's ever fucked me there, if that counts."

His tongue stops for a beat—oh, yes, maybe that counts—then resumes its torture.

Waves of hot pleasure and prickly embarrassment roll over me, twisting my mind upside down. I can't think straight when he's doing that, so I stop trying and just grip the blanket beneath me.

My orgasm comes quickly once he slides his hand up the inside of my thigh and finds my clit.

And as soon as that one fades, he's bodily moving me, first to the side, then once he has a condom, lifting me on top of him. I'm boneless, but that doesn't bother him in the least.

He's big and hard all over, muscles flexing as he spreads my legs and pushes into me. We both groan, a chorus of sex noises that sound foreign to me. Strange and wonderful. I bury my face in his neck, wanting more of his scent, more of his sweat as he begins to move inside me.

One of his hands holds my arms together behind my back.

The other curves over my ass, and as he fucks into me, he penetrates me there, too, filling both my holes with a ruthlessness that steals my breath.

I latch on to his neck, my mouth open and soft, and I lick up the taste of his sweat-slicked skin. His mouth presses against my temple, whispering frantic single words and phrases as he drives into me fast and furiously.

"Fucking tight. Yes. Squeeze me, babe. Take it. Take me so deep." His head drops back, stretching his neck open and I kiss my way up that strong, muscled column until I reach the limit of my reach because he's holding me down on top of him. I press my legs against his, but he chases me, thrusting into me from below like a savage beast.

My savage beast.

Mine.

The word explodes inside me, shattering me to pieces. He said it to me, but it was insane and ridiculous and the kind of madness that comes from the best sex of your life.

I know better.

And yet...*mine*. I lick him again as my entire body trembles in the remnants of my climax.

I know better.

I do.

He curls under me, every muscle contracting as he loses his

edge of control, then slams up, burying himself inside me in more ways than one.

In every way.

He shudders over and over again as he releases my arms, as he runs his hands up to my shoulders, sinking his fingers in my hair and bringing my mouth to his.

My hands shake as I touch him, as I cling and wonder how I'm ever going to let him go.

And even as that fear twists like a cornered snake inside me, I know I will. I'll have to.

I'm not allowed to have this.

I take it anyway.

For tonight, in secret.

I kiss him over and over again. I slide against his back as he gets rid of the condom, then drag him on top of me, wanting more of his flesh against mine. I push against his hands, urging him to hold me down, and when I feel him get hard again, I reach for a second condom and roll it down his length.

I'll take everything tonight.

———

"Why do you live in a hotel?"

I turn to the side and look at the red numbers on the clock. It's nearly four in the morning. "I don't."

He draws a lazy circle on my side. "Where do you live?"

"Elsewhere."

"In Seattle."

"So asking me wasn't necessary."

"I was being polite."

"You should try harder to pretend you don't know all my secrets."

"I don't know them all."

The rest of what he's thinking goes unsaid. *But he wants to.*

I roll onto my back and his hand slides over my hip and onto my belly. He spreads his fingers wide, finding my scar.

Neither of us say anything for a long while, but I hold still, and he holds me, and that's something in itself.

When I eventually turn toward him, his hand slips between my legs. We kiss, slow and languid, and in the distance, past the murky goodness of being turned on, I have a vague thought that I might write a song about this. About making love, dirty kisses and soft touches, and the way they crack you open.

We're way past the point of pretending this isn't something.

But what can survive the hellfire that is my life?

I pull my lips together, so our next kiss is firm and final. An end to dirty sexy times, because we need to talk.

So not my strong suit. I take a deep breath. "So this thing between us."

He brushes hair off my cheek. "Yes."

"You know what I'm going to say."

"I honestly have no idea. Is this about Grant?"

I make a face. "I was hoping to avoid that conversation."

"You don't need to." He grips my chin, gentle but firm, and brings his face right to mine. "Whatever it is, I'm going to deal with it."

Unwanted memories roll over me. "It's not that simple."

"It is for me. I see you. I like what I see. Every last inch of you. Secrets and pain. And I think you see me too." He frowns. "Or maybe you don't."

I search his face. "What do you mean?"

He traces along my jaw and down my neck. "I hacked into your phone."

"I know." And the crazy computer set up is intense, too. "And you're investigating Gerome Lively. I imagine you break the rules in that pursuit."

"I break the rules for a lot of reasons."

"What else?"

"To get things. Do things. See things."

"You're a...thief? Conman? Hacker?"

"Sure. Yes. Definitely."

"What else?"

"I used to work for the government."

"And not as a park ranger, I'm guessing."

"Never underestimate a park ranger." He rubs his thumb up and down at the base of my neck.

My pulse jumps against his touch. "Okay, so...a spy?"

"You could say that."

"You're making this whole secret-sharing thing difficult."

"It's like washing long, beautiful red hair. I've never done it before."

"I'm special?" I ask it lightly, but the way my heart beat races, I want it to be true.

His thumb presses into my skin. "Yes, you are."

I think he's earned a secret. "I ran away from home on my fifteenth birthday. Don't be sorry, either. It wasn't a home to mourn the loss of."

He doesn't blink.

"That's how I ended up in Seattle. Seemed like a decent place for a teenager to winter on the streets."

Still no reaction. That's good. If that broke him, I'd never get through the rest of it.

I take a deep breath. "It didn't take Grant long to find me. And he changed my life."

"But you hate him."

"Yes."

"What did he do you?"

I can't say it. Instead, I take his hand and press it to my belly.

Under my fingers, his muscles tighten. His entire body goes tense, coiling tight, and I start to shake.

"You were fifteen?"

I nod.

He wants to ask more questions, but I can't. And as the tears start to fall, silent, wet slides of regret and anguish, he cups my face in his hands and kisses each of them away, until his face is just as wet as mine.

"I'll take that secret to my grave," he whispers against my mouth. "You have nothing to fear from me."

"I have everything to fear. From you, because of you..." My breath hitches, but I get it under control. "Mostly from myself. I have a lot to fear about my own impulses and desires."

He holds my face, not saying anything for an agonizingly long time, then he brushes his fingers through my hair. "I have no doubt that if you need to, you'll be able to walk away to protect yourself. And I want you to. Never put me before you, you understand that? I don't want that. I want you safe, no matter what."

"I need to tell you...the Grant thing."

"Another time."

"The marriage is real."

"Do I look like a guy who gives a fuck about technicalities?"

"I..."

"Are you out of protests?"

I don't know what to say to that.

He holds me in silence, maybe until he knows I'm not going to say anything else. "Once a month I'll find you. I'll try to limit the amount of contact in between."

"That thing on my phone?"

"It's not traceable. Nobody will know I'm reaching out to you."

"You can't."

"I can. Nobody will know."

"That's not possible."

"Oh, babe. No. Actually, anything is possible." He kisses my forehead. "And we're going to take advantage of all of it."

My head is spinning. For the first time in a decade, I feel a weird kind of hope. It's got a crazy number of strings attached to it, and it feels fragile as fuck, but...this might just work. I might get to have this, at least for a little while.

I lean in close and brush my lips against his skin. "For the next time we get together, you should know I can't get pregnant."

He swallows hard. "Good to know. I'll make sure to get you an up-to-date health check."

Holy shit. I grin. "I'll do the same."

[20]

WILSON

NEW YORK

AUGUST

When I get back from L.A., we're suddenly slammed with work. Apparently the lazy heat of summer means people make bad decisions and do stupid things.

But when Tabitha schedules a twenty-four hour trip to New York, there's no question I'm going to make time to see her.

I'm pretty mobile. I run a dark web browser on my phone that lets me connect to my private servers, and in turn, any of the monitoring I've got set up. Right now, that's just Tabitha's. Before I left, I gave her a few things. An ereader with a secret built-in browser, a GPS tracker, and a few apps on her phone that looked innocuous but allowed her to message me if she needed to.

She didn't for three weeks.

I have the patience of a fucking saint.

But then she gave me the heads up about the trip, even before her credit card was used to book the flight.

At some point I'm going to have to stop lurking in her digital footprint like a tech-perv.

Not today, though.

Not any time soon, either, because I don't trust Derew as far as I could throw him while he was weighted down with a lead full-body cast.

It is some fucked-up bullshit to trap a teenager in a weird psuedo-marriage in order to control her career. And there might be more to it than that—the thought makes me ball my fists in rage—but no amount of theorizing spits out an explanation that's not disgusting.

My bots are searching for him, though. If he drifts the wrong direction on the internet, they'll find him.

And in the meantime, I have a date with his wife.

003-3000: Where are you?

Tabitha: Lord & Taylor on Fifth Ave. But I bet you know that already.

003-3000: You always rain on my attempts to be polite.

Tabitha: Are you here already?

003-3000: Ten minutes away.

Tabitha: I'll meet you on the main floor.

She's on her phone when I step inside from the sweltering heat. I stop and look at her. She's wearing a floral dress under a tiny denim vest and knee-high lace-up platform sandals. Her hair is piled on top of her head and she has an oversized bag slung over one shoulder.

She looks like a teenager, like an innocent little rebel, and a flash of anger stabs through me before I can lock it down. She never really got to be that innocent little rebel in real life.

Neither did I, though, and we both fucking survived, so the sentimentality isn't necessary.

I find myself needing to harden my heart far too often lately. It's a strange sensation, that softness in my chest. I don't like it.

But then she looks up and gives me a playful smile, and I'm mush again.

I'll go back to being heartless in eighteen hours.

"Hey," she says as I stop in front of her.

There's a calculated risk in being in public, but nothing I've looked at indicates that her manager is having her followed or watched in any way. He wouldn't know where to start to effectively do it, either.

So I kiss her. I reach out and pull her to me, one arm wrapped all the way around her waist, the other hand holding the back of her neck, and I kiss the fucking daylights out of her.

She tastes faintly of peppermint gum and wet, sweet promise. I'm going to have her mouth on my dick the second we're alone, then I'll repay the favour by burying my face between her legs until she screams.

She tastes like sex because that's what we've got, that's what we're allowed to miss, but my arms tighten around her, just kissing her, because damn it, I've missed *her*.

Fucking softness.

It'll be my death, but I'll die with a smile on my face.

"Where are we staying?" she asks when I let her up for air.

I'm at the same boutique hotel in SoHo she's at. "One floor down from your room."

"Why did I ask?" She shakes her head, but her eyes are sparkling.

"You look like you've had a good day."

She grinned. "Just signed a contract with a big tour promoter for a winter tour."

"That sounds like something one would celebrate."

"Right? Which is why I'm shopping. I'm looking for a dress to wear on the Ben & Emily show tomorrow morning."

"Did you find one?"

"Not yet. Do you mind if we go to Knight's across the road?"

"Lead the way."

Except I actually lead the way, because bodyguard tendencies come naturally to me, and it bothers me that she doesn't use them. She never has, from what I can tell. Instead she seems to cultivate an interesting dynamic with the paparazzi, giving them enough interesting B-roll when they want it that if she's doing something boring like shopping, they tend to leave her alone.

But there's nobody around when we hit the steaming sidewalk. We join the throngs of New Yorkers crossing the street, then head through the door opened for us by a uniformed doorman at Knight's.

It's just as fancy as any of the other stores on Fifth Avenue, but it's not a chain. Vaguely in the back of my mind, I know something about the company. Brothers own it, and two spun off their fortunes into tech.

Once we're inside, Tabitha takes the lead for real. She's been here before, and she strides with purpose toward the elevator; but she doesn't skip a beat when I curve my hand around her elbow and guide her to the stairs, instead.

"I don't take elevators I haven't had a chance to check out," I murmur in her ear.

"That's not paranoid or anything," she says with a smile.

"Better paranoid than dead."

"Touche."

"So I didn't really take you for a high fashion kind of girl."

"Woman."

"Apologies."

She laughs, a rolling giggle that makes her shoulders shake. "Oh, Wilson. And what kind of girl did you take me for?"

"A dirty one."

"In what kind of clothes?"

"No clothes." I shake my head. Obviously. "I don't know. I assumed all angsty rock stars shopped at...thrift stores?"

She stops at the top of the stairs and gives me the biggest grin. "You'd totally go to Goodwill with me, wouldn't you?"

Fucking hell, I'd go to church craft sale for her. "In a heartbeat."

"Good. But sometimes I do this, too. Want to watch me try things on?"

"Hell, yeah."

She's got a really specific taste, and spends more time nope-ing dresses still on the rack than pulling things off to consider. But she's quick, too, and it doesn't take long before she has four contenders and is being guided to a private change room by a very solicitous sales woman.

"Would your...would you like to have a seat?" she asks me, after starting to ask Tabitha and aborting hard. Do we look that mismatched? I'm wearing a suit today, because I dropped by Federal Plaza this morning to touch base with an FBI agent acquaintance, and they tend not to let hackers through the door unless they look like lawyers.

"I need his advice," Tabitha says with a slow wink. "You know how it is."

"Of course, Ms. Leyton." And nothing more was said on the matter.

I wait to react until we're in the...small sitting room, essentially. It has a firm-looking couch across from the mirror, and that's where I sit. I loosen my tie.

"She knows you," I say.

"I was here two hours ago. I bought a dress for three thousand dollars. That's the kind of thing you remember."

"I bet. So why are we back?"

She peels off her denim vest and tips her head to the side. "Because this room is private and I thought you might want to watch me try on some dresses."

———

"You are officially a spoilsport," she says as I haul her into my hotel room. We stopped by her room long enough to forward her phone down here.

Now she's all mine, and after the last hour of fucking fantastic torture—stripping, teasing, grinding, and a nearly successful plea for me to just take her there on that couch—I have payback to dispense.

On her ass.

In her ass.

I press her against the wall and kiss her savagely as I hike up her skirt, my palm searching for that hot little pussy that begged to be taken in public.

I cover her panties, finding her clit with the heel of my hand as my fingers squeeze around her sex. "You are a bad, bad influence."

"Me?" She grins wickedly. "Like you've never fucked in public."

"Never where there might be video cameras, no."

"There aren't any in those change rooms. That's against the law."

"The law?" I bite her lower lip until she gasps. "That has nothing to do with it. Blackmail, humiliation, maybe just someone who wants to get off on it..."

"But you didn't stop me from teasing you."

"I have a signal disrupter in my phone case that scrambles most modern tech. But the point remains, it's a bad idea. Not to mention sex with you is never tidy or quiet. I don't want to have to make a mess for a salesperson to clean up."

"Oh, noble sir—"

I slap my hand against the inside of her thigh. "Nothing noble about me. You want me to fuck you in a change room? I can give you that now. Wait. Right. Here."

This place is way swankier than the shitty hotel room I had in L.A., and from the second she started her little show at Knight's, I knew what I wanted to do with her when we got back here.

There's a big-ass antique mirror in the corner, next to the window. I move the oversized upholstered chair from the other corner and position it in front of the mirror.

Then I stalk back to where Tabitha is leaning against the wall, grinning at me, and I hoist her onto my shoulder. With my free hand, I pick up her shopping bag from Knight's.

She shrieks as I carry her across the room, but her protest turns to a sweet little moan when I set her down in front of the mirror.

"Try on the red one," I tell her, my voice rasping.

My dick is hard enough to pound nails as I settle into the chair.

She stands in the space between me and the mirror and repeats the same stripping routine that got me so hard when we were on Fifth Avenue.

It would have the same affect now if I weren't already threatening the seams of my suit pants.

She pulls her dress off, then reaches for the new purchase.

"Lose the panties," I growl.

She skims her fingertips over her tattoo and notches her

thumbs on the skinny side pieces. "You're not supposed to try on clothes without your underwear on," she says, biting her lip.

I grin. "I'll buy the dress, guaranteed. Now show me your pussy. And remember to be quiet. We don't want the sales girl to hear us."

She presses her lips together, quiet as a church mouse, and gets herself naked. Then she smoothes the red dress over her her body. The deep vee in front plunges almost to her navel, and the asymmetrical hem goes down to her sandals on one side, but cuts high on her thigh on the other.

It's perfect.

She's perfect.

"You like this one best?"

"I really do. Come here." I pull her into my lap, nestling her ass against my straining dick. "Let me see you."

I don't mean the dress.

I mean her curves, her cunt, every last inch of her sexy-as-sin body.

Mine.

First I brush along the inner swells of her breasts, raising goosebumps I want to cover with jizz. I want her on her knees, begging for me to mark her with my seed.

All in good time.

The neckline peels back, baring her breasts. Her head falls back beside mine and I kiss her jaw, wet and hot.

"Eyes on the mirror," I whisper as I move my hands, palms flat, up and over them. Her nipples are hard little pebbles. "You are so fucking sexy," I mutter, watching her watch me. "Look at how hard your nipples are. I bet you're soaking wet for my already, aren't you?"

She bites her lower lip and nods, her entire body trembling.

I ghost my hands down her body, heading for that hemline, and when I find it, I curl my fingers around the fabric. Her thighs are smooth and warm, and my head begins to buzz as I crawl the skirt up her legs, rubbing her skin with my knuckles the whole way to her hips.

In the mirror, we both watch as I bare her cunt, our role-play that of an illicit, time-sensitive fuck in a change room.

But I could hold her on my lap like this for hours and just look at her.

She's not having any of that.

"Please, Wilson..." She tangles her fingers with mine and pulls our hands between her legs.

I watch in the mirror as we touch her pussy together.

"I need you here," she whispers. "I feel empty. We can be quick."

Lust jolts through me. My tongue feels thick as I curl my body around hers, pulling her legs wider still. "Want me to fill you up?"

"Yes." She rocks on her thighs, lifting herself up and making space for me to unzip behind her.

My cock bounces against her ass as I get my pants out of the way, then I fit us together easily. She's tight, wet and ready for me. Being bare against her is like an electric current, and I want more, but I want it slow. I don't want to miss a single moment of this first slide into her without anything between us.

"Yes, yes, yes...." She pants as I pulse my hips, stretching her entrance. "Put it in me."

"Shhh..." I ease her onto me—Jesus, nothing in the world feels this good—then guide her up and down with one hand while the other finds her clit. Already hard and swollen, it fits perfectly between two fingertips. I drive into her, pushing her into my hand at the same time as I pinch my fingers together.

She gasps, and I do it again.

Hard, fast, rough.

Her hip is going to have a red handprint from where I'm gripping her.

Good. I want to mark her in a thousand ways, inside and out.

My dick thickens even more, stretching her out as I ruthlessly make her ride me all the way down. My pulse pounds in my neck as I bottom out inside her, my bare cock snug insider her cunt.

This is how it's supposed to be. Fuck my life that I didn't know this before, but holy hell, I'm gonna hang on to this woman forever. I swear under my breath, and she moans, "yes, forever, fuck me," and it feels too fucking good to worry about how much of that I said out loud.

"Wilson," she says desperately, her voice rising as she chases the orgasm I'm pounding into her.

I've never cared about my name before now, but fuck, that sounds right. "Yes, secret girl. Come on my cock. Come on, that's a good girl. Fuck yeah."

I bury myself inside her, holding still as she pulses around me, and when she tips over the edge, I cover her mouth to keep up the pretense of this being dirty changing room sex.

But fuck, it stopped being that somewhere in the middle of me losing my mind.

I hold her tight, breathing her in as she shudders in my arms, and when the last after-shocks of her orgasm fade, I ease her off my still-raging cock.

But my secret girl doesn't share my plans to save that for later. She spins around and sinks to her knees, her eyes wide and her cheeks pink. Her tits are still out and they're fucking glorious. She's still right in the role-play, no problem. "I think we've got another minute. Can you come quickly?"

"Fuck. Yes." I fist the base of my cock as she swallows my length, her lips stretching wide. It's an obscene image, her on her knees for me, working her way up and down my still-wet-from-her pole. My balls are tight and my release is already churning, ready to explode onto her tongue. "Suck me. Harder. Yes."

I'm whispering guttural nothings now as her tongue slides against my throbbing skin. She's perfect, my dirty little secret. Filthy perfection.

When I come, the corners of my vision go black and I see spots. She swallows every spurt, and sits back on her heels when I finish shooting down her throat.

"Yummy," she whispers, licking her lips, and I die all over again.

[21]
TABITHA

When I wake up, it's dark outside and Wilson is awake, working at the desk. He has two laptops open.

In the glow of the screens, he looks serious. Intent.

I don't say anything, but it doesn't take him long to realize I'm awake and looking at him. He glances over. "You're awake."

"So are you."

"Did I wake you? I don't sleep much."

"No, it's fine." I stretch my arms above my head, then push myself up to a sitting position. "I'm kind of hungry?"

He points to the mini-fridge. "I went out and got some Japanese soba noodles, a green salad, grilled chicken, and some sticky dessert balls that smell like cherry blossoms."

I crawl out of bed and check out the food. He bought enough to feed a small army. I assemble a plate for myself. "Do you want me to dish you up some as well?"

He waves his hand. "I'll get some in a little bit, if that's okay. I'm in the middle of something."

So I sit cross-legged on the bed, naked, and eat while I watch him. He doesn't seem distracted by the intense observation, either.

When I finish my midnight dinner, I go to the bathroom to wash up. There's a new toothbrush next to the sink and a bottle of the Icelandic skin cream that I use, too. I could have just brought my stuff down from upstairs, or for that matter invited him to share my room with me, but there's something about this that I get the sense Wilson needs. Like he's providing for me.

I like it.

Nobody has ever really done that before. I have people on my payroll who do it because I compensate them extraordinarily well. But I need to tell them what I want, how I like things. Without a single prompt, Wilson got food that he knew I'd enjoy,

He's still at the computer when I come out of the bathroom. I move to his side, and he holds out his arm, pulling me into his lap. He's wearing boxer briefs and a fitted t-shirt that I want to strip off of him, but he's working, so I resist the temptation to distract him with sex.

For now.

I peek at the screen. "Wow, there's a lot going on in the middle of the night."

He points at one corner, where three columns of what look like chatrooms are scrolling. "It's not the middle of the night in Russia." Then he points to a bigger black square in the middle. "And when the rest of America is sleeping is a good time for me to go peeking inside their systems."

"That's..."

"Creepy?" I can feel him smiling.

"Intense." It really doesn't feel creepy. I can feel his heartbeat where my arm is wrapped around his chest, and it's slow and steady, although from the hints he's given me, I think that's more due to training than anything else. But it's not creepy because *he* isn't. I twist my head toward him so I can see his face. "Thank you for finding my face cream. That was really sweet."

He gives me a half-smirk. "Easy to notice what you like when I'm spying on you."

"You'd be surprised how many people I spend every day with who don't notice things like that."

"That's a real shame. But I'm not surprised." His mouth tightens as his eyes flick back to the screen. "People prove just how selfish they are every single day."

I laugh weakly. "I thought that was just Hollywood."

He shakes his head absently. "You have no idea." Then he huffs out a breath and kisses my head. "And I don't want you to, either. I think I want some of that food now. And then we can find a movie or something to watch and make out like teenagers."

[22]

TABITHA

LOS ANGELES

OCTOBER

"Over here, Tabitha!"

"Who are you wearing?"

"Show us some thigh!"

I brush my hand across the split in my steampunk inspired ball gown and strike a pose for the photographers on the red carpet. This is my third year attending this black-tie fundraiser for LAST. Los Angeles Sexual assaulT, the step-and-repeat banner behind me spells out. A stark name for an agency dedicated to survivors of sexual violence in all forms.

Last year, I gave them an anonymous donation for a million dollars. That's how I balance out spending an embarrassing amount of money on dresses and tequila.

My public appearance here is just as much about ramping up toward the winter tour as it is an act of goodwill. "Do you like the dress?" I wink at the videographer from TMZ. "It's going to be on the cover of my new album, that's how much I love it!"

"When does that come out, Tabitha?"

"Next month." Big smile, bright eyes. "It's gonna be *hot*."

I say the same thing to the People Online reporter, and the guy from Music Station who always stares at my tits like they're going to invite him in for a motorboat.

Never going to happen, dude.

By the time I get inside, my smile is stiff and my cheeks hurt, so I head straight for the bar. The first one is in the hallway outside the ballroom, near the coat check, but a helpful hostess points out that there's another bar set up on the far side, so I bee-line there, and that hallway—which leads to the kitchen and prep areas of the hotel—is empty.

All except for one man, handsome and tall in a tux and a half-smirk.

I skid to a stop. "What are you doing here?"

Wilson shrugs. "Wanted to have a drink with you."

"You didn't text."

"You didn't either." He gestures to the bar, and we place our orders. I want a shot of a tequila and a lemon water. He wants a beer.

In September, I'd returned to New York again, and we'd spent another day and a half in the SoHo hotel. It had been exactly as good as in August, and there was no good reason why I hadn't reached out to him to see when he might be heading this way, or if I should head that way...but I didn't.

"I figured you'd worry about that," I say lamely. It's not true. I'm scared of how intense this is between us. How he's all I can think about much of the time, and how I feel when I'm with him —like I'm a completely different person.

One I like a hell of a lot more than the person I am the rest of the time.

But I don't need to go to therapy to know that's unhealthy. I can't hook all of my dreams of my life changing on Wilson. That's not anywhere near reality. That's a fantasy I'm way too jaded to let myself indulge in.

The bartender sets my shot in front of me and I take it like the pro I am.

Wilson watches with an amused look on his face as I take a quick suck at the lime wedge that came on the side.

"And worry about it I did." He winks. "Actually, this is a work trip. I'll be back in a few weeks, but a case we've been working on for a long time has come to a head and that's why I'm in L.A."

Oh.

Shit, I'm the worst kind of self-absorbed bitch for thinking he was only here for me.

"But seeing you is the highlight of my entire month," he says softly after we get our other drinks. He cups his hand around my elbow and leads me into the ballroom again. The way the room is set up, there are tables all over the place, with no assigned seating, and there's a dance floor at one end. At the other are displays about LAST, and this is where he guides me. He takes our drinks and sets them on a ledge running along the wall as the DJ slows down the music.

He gives me a serious look. "Last time I was out here, I had to watch you dance from the shadows."

"And tonight?"

He holds out his hand. "Maybe you could join me in the shadows. May I have the honor?"

My heart pounds as I slide my fingers over his.

He folds me against his body, warmth radiating off him as he begins to turn us in a slow, meandering circle. "I can't stay for long. I have to fly back to D.C. tonight."

"Okay." My voice does a shitty job of masking how much I don't like that.

He presses his cheek to my temple, and I'm grateful for the ridiculous heels bringing me closer to his height. "Next month."

I nod silently, disappointment sliding through me. This is a warning sign. *Danger. Getting too attached.* "I like the tux, by the way."

"It serves a purpose."

"More than just seeing me?"

He hesitates. "Yes."

I probably can't ask what that other mission is. So I change the subject because all I want to care about in this moment is how good it feels to dance with him. "This is nice, though."

"It is." He kisses my temple and his arm tightens around my waist.

"Tell me something," I whisper.

"Like what?"

"Anything. Something surprising."

He leans back enough to look at me. His eyes are crinkling at the corners, like he knows he's actually going to surprise me. He does. "I know how to knit."

I laugh in delighted surprise. "You do not."

"I do."

"How?"

"A client taught me."

"A woman?"

His mouth tightens as he gives me a hard look. "A client."

"Okay."

"There's nobody else."

"I know." I hesitate. "The same, you know."

"I do."

Obviously, we'd exchanged health reports and the promise was implicit there, but jealousy was on a whole other level.

I take a deep breath. "Knitting. Huh. What else do you know how to do?"

"Everything." He says it lightly, but there's a hint of a challenge in the back, faint as can be. I wonder if anyone else has ever noticed that he worries he might not be good enough.

"I have no doubt," I say softly. "I'm impressed."

He smirks. "Sure."

Oh, no. Challenge accepted. I'm going to prove to Mr. Tough Guy that I really am impressed. "Teach me how to knit."

He shrugs. "Yeah."

"No, I mean it."

The music changes, but he doesn't let me go. "Where are you going to be next month?"

"I'm going home for a few weeks before we start rehearsing for tour."

He steps back, deftly sweeping up my hand as he moves. He kisses my fingers, then gives me a serious look. "Then I'll come to you, and I'll bring some wool."

SEATTLE

NOVEMBER

As soon as I'm able, I take four days off and fly to Seattle. I rent a car at Sea-Tac Airport under an alias, and arrive at her place mid-afternoon. She has a three-car garage, and one of the doors opens as soon as I text her that I've arrived.

She opens the inside door and steps into the garage, backlit by the afternoon sun streaming through her house.

I don't know what to expect here. This is the first time we've done anything like this.

It'll be the first time we've done anything—other than shopping and a single dance—outside of a hotel room.

I've come prepared for anything.

Knitting lessons.

Kinky sex.

Sparring.

I'm kind of hoping we do all of the above.

But first, a kiss.

I drop my suitcase in front of her and she leaps into my arms. "Missed you," she whispers as I trace my fingers up her neck and spear them into her hair, holding her in place for my mouth to show her I feel exactly the same way.

She tastes sweet, like berries, and warm, like a turned-on woman.

I definitely came prepared for that, too. I have her shirt off before we're even inside. Her shorts are left on the floor of the hallway as she leads me, naked, to her bed.

"Nice room," I growl as I climb on top of her, jerking her thighs up and open for me. She's wet, slick and hot already, and I sink right into her.

She gasps and throws her head back.

"Nice house, too."

She giggles. "You didn't even see it."

"Okay, nice bed."

"Nicer with you in it," she whispers, tugging my weight down onto her. "Kiss me."

I slide my tongue along hers, curling and thrusting in time with my cock inside her cunt, and we come together in a fast, hurried climax.

When I roll to the side, I hold on to her, and pull her on top of me.

She exhales roughly and puts her cheek down on my chest.

"So..."

I can feel her smiling in reaction. "Yeah?"

"How was your week?"

"Busy." She yawns. "Rehearsals are going well, though. So that's good. And I went grocery shopping this morning so I've got food for us."

"Such luxury."

"I ate half of the strawberries, though."

"I tasted them," I say with a quiet laugh. "Were they good?"

"Amazing." She kisses my chest. "Almost as good as that delicious fuck, Mr. Carter. Shall we do it again?"

My cock leaps to life beneath her, and I set my hands on her hips, urging her back. She's sloppy from my first load, and fuck, but that's hot in a filthy way.

She squirms against my erection. "You like me on top?"

"Fucking right. I want to watch you writhe for me."

"I should show you the rest of my place..."

I thrust into her. Yes, being on the bottom is my favorite position. "All in good time."

———

The next thing I see is her bathroom, which is magnificent.

"This shower holds what, like ten people?"

She blushes, and I pin her against the tile wall.

"Really?"

She rolls her eyes. "You know how we are. Hedonistic Hollywood types. And it was tight at six."

I laugh and kiss a water droplet off her lower lip. "I bet."

"It was a few years ago. When I bought the place. Housewarming party got kind of out of control. I don't usually...here."

"It's fine," I whisper, and the kiss gets deeper.

The sun is setting when we finally make it to the kitchen. The west-facing side of her house is almost entirely windows, letting in a stunning view of Puget Sound, and an island in the near distance.

She's made up some plates of finger foods, mostly fruits and vegetables, but some meat and dips and crackers, too. We carry them outside, where she has a fancy heater for the deck, and a box of blankets.

I pull her into my lap and we lazily eat while we talk and watch the sun drop out of sight on the horizon.

"This feels like we're playing house," I muse as we tidy up in the kitchen.

She shoots me a weird look. "Is that a bad thing?"

I frown. "No." Did I make it sound like it was?

"Is it a good thing?" She laughs. "Want me to get a 1950's style dress and cook you a meatloaf?"

"Forget I said anything."

"But you did. Why?"

"Because it's different than what we've done before, that's why. Leave it alone."

"Or what, you'll spank me for questioning the master of the house?"

I raise my eyebrows at her. "That's an interesting direction to take it."

She rinses her hands, then slowly dries them on a towel hanging on her stove. "Come on. Let's go to bed and watch a late-night comedy show."

"How domestic." I swat her bottom, and we do just that, but the exchange continues to sting at the back of my mind.

The next morning we make waffles, then workout together in her home gym. I teach her how to take me down to the mat, and she teaches me how to sing and run on a treadmill at the same time.

After lunch we're being kind of nappy together on the couch when her phone vibrates, and I grab it off the coffee table and hand it to her. "Someone who doesn't know how to make your phone magically ring wants your attention," I whisper against her neck.

She giggles and takes it, but she kisses me first before looking at the message. A good, dirty kiss that gets me halfway hard.

But after she reads the message, she scrambles off me and starts to pace as she types a fast response. The scowl on her face deepens.

"What is it?" I stand, too, worry mounting.

She gives me a helpless look. "You have to leave for part of the day tomorrow. Grant's flying in with contracts."

It's the last thing I expect to hear. "Excuse me?"

"I didn't know he was coming. He just told me."

"How long will that take?"

"He'll stretch it out. It might take most of the afternoon." She has the good grace to wince, but I don't like this.

I really don't like this. "I'm only here for two more days."

"I can't tell him that."

"Yeah." But I don't sound like I understand, because I don't. Fuck it all to hell.

She follows me into the kitchen.

I ignore her as I pour a glass of water.

"I couldn't tell him no," she whispers, and I nod.

"Yeah, I heard you the first time."

"You knew this was the deal."

Reality has slammed back into me. We might be playing at domestic fun, but I'll always be a dirty secret. "Right."

"Wilson…"

I shake my head. "I get it. But I don't have to like it. I'll go out, it'll be fine."

But it isn't fine, and when she takes my hand and tugs me back into the living room to watch a movie, I pull her into my lap. I hold on tight, so fucking tight, and it doesn't make a difference.

I've fallen hard, stupid hard, for someone who can't belong to me.

She fucking belongs to me, but she doesn't at the same time, and I lost sight of that along the way.

The responsible, mature thing to do would be to get over it.

Instead, I stew all night.

When we fuck, it's hard and rough. I hold her down and she pushes against me, her eyes on fire. I slam the first spurt of my seed deep inside her, hot and scalding, then pull out and mark her with the rest.

A white rope of come across her belly. *Mine.*

Another shot across the swell of her tits. *Mine.*

The last one catches her chin and drips onto her neck. *My fucking woman.*

She rubs it all in, every last drop, but then climbs out of bed and walks silently into the shower.

I don't join her.

It's dawn when I admit I'm not going to sleep.

I roll out of bed and sit, legs wide, head in my hands.

I feel her stir behind me and I don't turn around until she says my name.

"Wilson..."

I glare at her. "Is this all you want from me?"

"I can't..." She stiffens, then lifts her chin and looks me right in the eye. "Yes. This is all I want. This is what works for me. And this was the deal. I don't want any more than this."

It's a damn lie. And we both know that this isn't the end of anything, that I'll be back for her sooner than later. But right now? I don't want to see her face a single second more. "Then you don't get me."

I'm shaking as I do the one thing I swore I'd never do, and walk away from her.

[24]
TABITHA

SEATTLE

DECEMBER

CHRISTMAS DAY

I don't hear from him for a month.

The silence is deafening, and deep inside, I can feel myself unspooling because of it.

Turns out there's something worse than love. I can't even name it, exactly, but what Wilson has unlocked by dragging me back to that buried pain has made me reckless.

Now I'm reminded constantly of that fleeting awakening when I finally, desperately knew what it was to love another person, only to have him snatched from me. Too small, too new, too fragile for this world.

Not Wilson, though. Nothing about him is small or fragile. But I lost him anyway, by the bonds of my own making.

I lost him, but...

I know he's watching. I have no doubt he's bugged my house top to bottom, and when I get back from Los Angeles, I hole up on the couch. In a weird way, that makes me feel a little closer to him, but I know I'm just deluding myself.

He'll keep an eye on me because he's noble, a dark knight, but I've wounded him.

And the worst part is, it's for the best. I'm about to go on tour. Grant will be there constantly and I wouldn't be able to easily hide a rendezvous.

We weren't going to last forever, I keep telling myself.

It feels wrong. It makes me sick to the pit of my stomach no matter how often I repeat it.

I punish myself on the treadmill and in my home gym. I do sit-ups until my stomach seizes up in protest. I run for miles, long past the point of my legs burning. I don't care.

When Grant comes by on his way to his parents', he tells me I look better than I have in ages. I want to punch him in the face.

"It'll be good to be fit for tour," I finally manage.

He doesn't ask me if I want to join them for Christmas dinner. I know I'm not welcome there, not that I'd accept the invitation anyway.

I'm not the little slut that ruined their son's life.

Exactly the opposite, not that I'd ever try to win that fight. They'd never hear it. People like them are too closed-minded to hear anything other than what they've already decided for themselves.

Well, fuck them. They can say a prayer for me to go to Hell when they go to Mass tonight. Joke's on them. I know God doesn't listen to bullshit like that.

Not when he's got my son by his side, whispering the truth.

When he leaves, I slam the door a little too hard behind him, and something inside me snaps.

I sag against it, my oversized Acacia wood door in my sprawling, beach-view mansion that will never have crayon on the walls or a plastic play kitchen in the real kitchen.

Maybe that's why I don't fucking use it.

An ugly, gross sob wells up in my chest, and I fight it hard.

No, I tell myself. Fuck off with that sadness. It's been a long year. A long decade. And I've done my share of grieving, but this feels different.

This feels like it might actually break me if I let it out.

I can't break now. I gave up Wilson. I gave up the only goodness I'd allowed myself, to keep everything tight and controlled.

The sob didn't care. It ripped out of me, coming out a wounded howl, and I crumpled to floor as another followed. I relived every moment in the hospital, from waking up in Emergency to being transferred to Labour & Delivery.

They shouldn't call it that when your baby is dead.

They shouldn't let you go there when you killed your baby, even if you're a baby yourself.

There are some things that are unforgivable, for which they should just send you straight to the morgue.

Familiar guilt swirls over me like a fog. I can hear myself sobbing, but it's in the distance. There's ringing, too, but I ignore it. I give in to the fog until it swamps me fully, until I'm limp and lifeless on the cold tile of the entranceway.

Eventually the sobbing stops, and I think, oh, she's done.

Good, she doesn't deserve grief.

Then the ringing starts again, this time different.

This time it's my song.

Did I tell you I loved you
Enough times for you to remember
Won't make it to heaven, though
So you're on your own there, love

But you'll be fine
You'll fly
You've got wings I'll never have
You'll fly
So carry my dreams, love
And you'll be fine
You'll fly

I push myself onto all fours, then stand. Unsteady, I follow it until I find the source—my phone, and the screen is flashing.

I answer the call, but I don't say anything.

"You're crying," Wilson finally mutters.

"I've been crying for weeks."

"Not like this."

"No."

"What is it? What did he do?"

I couldn't tell him before. But I've lost him already. He already knows I'm selfish. And maybe this is the punishment I'm looking for tonight.

So I tell him. I tell him about Keegan, and I start to cry all over again.

[25]

WILSON

I LISTEN, rage growing inside me, as Tabitha haltingly shares what happened when she was fifteen. I'm so mad at myself for not being there, for being a five-hour flight away, but I've been watching her for months now. I know she's a fighter. I know she doesn't need me.

But God fucking damn, I want to be there.

She might not be able to tell me all of this in person, though. She couldn't when we were together before.

I grip my phone so tight it occurs to me I might crack the casing, and I lean in toward the computer screen in front of me until I'm close enough that all I can see is her.

She's moved to the couch. She's sitting right in the middle, stiff as a statue.

"I didn't know I was pregnant at first. I was stupidly innocent about sex. He was the first guy I'd gone all the way with, and he always pulled out. So when I got sick and messed up a studio session he'd lined up for me, I felt bad. I went to a walk-in clinic and paid cash for my appointment. I told them I had the flu. They made me pee in a cup."

The pause here is longer than in between the other sentences.

"I didn't tell him right away," she whispers.

Fuck. Fuck, fuck, fuck. *No, of course you didn't, baby girl,* I want to say.

"I wasn't showing, and they said it was so small, just a walnut. I'll never forget that description. A walnut inside me. Then a plum. I found a website that showed me the size of the baby, and every week I would go and look it up. There was an email sign-up, and I couldn't fill it out because Grant might see it."

I've done the mental math before, and I've never liked it, but now I'm shaking with white-hot anger at a twenty-two-year-old fuck face who would terrify his fifteen-year-old girlfriend to the point where she was afraid to get emails about her pregnancy.

"And then we got another break. Someone we knew had to back out of a spotlight on local indie musicians, and Grant got me the spot. He wanted it for himself, but they wanted a female singer-songwriter. I was really tired that day, and he gave me something. For energy, he said."

On the screen, her shoulders shake, but it's silent over the phone.

Maybe this is too much. Maybe I've pushed her to tell me.

"I'm sorry," I say, my voice cracking.

She shakes her head.

"You didn't know you couldn't trust him." I want to tell her more. I want to tell her that nothing she will tell me will change how I feel about her, but she doesn't need that pressure right now. She doesn't need to bear the weight of how much I love her when her heart is lost forever.

I get it now. I thought we were the same. I thought we were both so broken that love wasn't possible.

But I'm broken because I'd never loved anyone, not in that formative way that teaches us how and who to fall in love with.

She's broken because she's loved with her entire being and it wasn't enough.

"I should have known," she finally whispers. "I should have protected him."

I wait. I don't know what she did or didn't do.

It doesn't matter.

She was a baby herself, in over her head.

"Keegan started moving inside me, or I started feeling him move inside me, the same day we got offered a recording deal. And that night, we...celebrated. I didn't drink anything, I claimed I was still under the weather, but Grant wanted...he fucked me that night. That was the last time we ever...And he felt my baby move. His hand was on my stomach and he felt something, and he put it all together.

"Everything moved quickly at that point. His parents are devoutly religious, and he told them. They insisted we get married. I was too young for that, but they knew a judge, and made a petition for an exception due to the pregnancy."

She's given me enough information that I'd be able to find her real life identity if I went looking for it. Even as I tell myself to let it go, the data churn begins.

That my mind goes there is probably reason enough for her not to trust me with this story, but I'm in now. I'm in deep, and I'm in forever. I don't care who she once was. I do care that her connection to that baby was stolen from her, though. I care about that with every fiber of my being.

Grant's identity wasn't created at age twenty-two. Why isn't the marriage in his background file?

"Wilson?" Her voice wavers.

"I'm here. You can keep going if you want. I'm not going

anywhere. I'm listening." And thinking, God help me. "What happened next?"

"Everything happened so quickly. We were married a few weeks later, then we flew to L.A. and we started using these names from the start there. Grant said it would be better if nobody knew we were married, because of the age difference, and he was right. He said once I really started showing, I'd go back to Seattle and we'd make it work somehow.

"Like an idiot, I believed him. And it seemed to work at first. The record execs were all over me. It was a lot to take in, a lot to handle. Grant made it really clear we weren't making any deals just yet. But he wanted them lined up for when we got back, and when I'd get run down, he'd give me a pill to keep me going."

Her voice is straining now, but she hasn't moved from her spot on the couch. I change cameras so I can see her from another angle. She's twisting her hands together, and something inside me twists with them.

"Four weeks after we arrived in California, there was a party." Her voice chills, the words sharpening, and I want to tell her to stop, it's okay, I don't need to know this part. But she needs to say it, so I want to listen. She needs a witness and I can be that for her. "There were producers and radio people there, label execs. It was at a big converted warehouse. Competing DJs, lots of drugs. We didn't get there until midnight, and I was exhausted. He gave me one pill, then another. I knew I shouldn't take the second one. I remember that thought so clearly. It was the first thing I said when I woke up. It was only later that the rest of the night came back to me. Flashes of people in front of me, offers of other drugs. I said no, no, no. I kept saying that, over and over again, and the party kept going. I was there until early morning, and at some point..."

She trails off.

I wait.

When she starts again, her voice is pure ice. "I did a line of cocaine. I can see myself in the bathroom. Another flash. Then an ambulance ride, and waking up in Emergency. I said, 'I didn't want it.' I meant the pills. I didn't know the rest, not until later. Someone said they couldn't find a heartbeat, and then it was a blur again."

This silence stretches so long I think she's done.

She's not.

"He was born sleeping, they said. He'd had a cardiac arrest inside me. I killed him. They cut me open to try and save his life. And when they told me he was gone, I wanted them to keep cutting me until I was a million pieces of nothing, because I didn't deserve to be alive if he wasn't."

"You didn't kill him." I know it's not what she wants to hear. I can't say anything she wants to hear. I can only speak the truth, as impotent as it is. "You didn't. Fucking hell, Tabitha, tell me that you know that now."

"I don't. And you can't...please don't. Others have tried. I'm not suicidal, I'm not a danger to myself. But I know what I did and I will never let myself live without that guilt."

"Why are you still with him?"

For the first time since I called her, she looks around the room, wondering where my invisible eyes are. She scans past me, and I clear my throat.

"Back a little to the left. The clock."

She gives me a rueful smile and leans back against the couch. "Because if I leave him, he'll tell the world I murdered my baby. He has video of me doing that line of cocaine in the bathroom. There was a time when I wanted him to expose me, but I can't do that to Keegan's memory. Right now he's my private angel. If people know about him, they'll find his grave.

They'll say disgusting things about his memory. And it will taint all the things I've quietly done to remember him."

"You said you can't have children..."

Her face twists. "God's idea of justice, maybe. Something went wrong during the operation when they tried to save his life. I had messed up cycles for a while after, and then my body gave up trying. It's for the best."

"How long after that did you start over?"

"We have that in common, don't we?" Her lips twist in a cold smile. "Not long at all. Grant was all prepared for it. Fucking bastard said it was for the best that we'd lost the baby. A week later, he'd somehow formalized these new identities for us. He was no longer Grant Rook, but Grant Derew, and I was Tabitha Leyton for real, not just a stage name."

Like the barrels of a lock sliding into place, my brain spun that information around until it clunked up against something else I knew.

Grant Rook.

Youngest son of Malcolm Rook, a rancher in Washington State.

Brother of Spencer Rook, who is on our firm's radar as a rising star in the white nationalist movement.

Grant Rook died ten years earlier.

How did he just ghost right there in plain view standing behind one of the country's biggest pop stars?

I stare at the screen.

Tabitha has no idea who she's married to.

But I do now.

And everything has just changed.

[26]
WILSON

CHRISTMAS NIGHT

I STAY on the phone with my secret girl until she falls asleep. Then I take the tablet into the main space and I prop it on the kitchen counter so I can keep an eye on her while I figure this out.

Most of her details I know by heart.

Her tour dates.

I grab a thick black marker and pace to the wall.

Los Angeles

San Francisco

Portland

Salt Lake City

Denver

Albuquerque
Phoenix

I write the dates next to the cities. There's a gap of five days between Portland and Salt Lake City. She's planning on going home to Seattle while the buses go on ahead and everyone gets a day off in Vegas.

Vegas.

I scrawl that in the middle.

Vegas always has potential to fuck someone up. And if Tabitha's safely out of the way, all the better.

I scrawl Grant's name at the far end of the wall. How do I get you the fuck away from my woman, you disgusting sack of shit?

His mostly estranged family is one option. I need to dig deeper into their backgrounds, and figure out who helped him with the new identities.

A new thought pulls me up short.

Could he have acquired the identities from the Feds?

I don't like that idea at all. I put the marker down and head back to my computer. If it was a US Marshall, it wouldn't have been official. Where to start searching for a ten-year-old cold lead on a corrupt government agent?

But it doesn't take me long to set that theory aside, because the Feds don't recycle social security numbers. And Grant Derew was a real kid. Two years older than Grant Rook, he was a California native who studied at UCLA, then worked in the Valley for the regional government until he went missing six months before Tabitha moved to Los Angeles—and then was quietly removed from the Missing Persons registry seven months later.

So whoever helped them trolled through that registry of missing people, found someone that Grant could be—right down to the first name—but no easy identity to adopt for Tabitha.

I pace back to the wall and draw a tall, skinny rectangle around Grant.

He's my last domino.

How do I get him to tip over?

Who can I set up to push him?

I write some names around him. His family. Silent business partners. Hollywood types.

None of the relationships are particularly strong, though.

What's his carrot?

What would he do anything for?

Grant got me the spot. He wanted it for himself, but they wanted a female singer-songwriter.

I spin around and grab the tablet. She's still asleep. I open a new window and search for Grant Rook performances. There he is, skinny kid, big head, real talent.

I don't feel any sympathy for him, nor does he deserve any, but this helps. Tabitha's a proxy. I need to give him another proxy—and then take it away, because there's no reward for being evil. Not if I can help it.

A falling from grace in public would make me happy, but it can't touch Tabitha.

Vegas.

A falling from grace in the underground would work, too.

Time to set up a fight for Nix in Sin City.

Dirty Love

part four

dirty deeds

WILSON

PRESENT DAY, AGAIN

WASHINGTON

FEBRUARY

I'VE ROUTED the live feeds from the Tabard Inn to our conference room. Tag is in charge of picking which mic we listen to the audio from, because I'm recording them all separately so it doesn't matter, and my bots will flag us if anything interesting is said anywhere in the building.

They'll also flag me privately if Tabitha's name comes up anywhere, for any reason.

I don't expect it to, but after the last month, it's been on my mind that Spencer Rook might have opinions about his sister-in-law.

He's never spoken about her in his online screeds. And in the conversations we've had since Christmas about Grant, when I've carefully led her toward his family, she's never mentioned his brother contacting her. She knows I know more about Grant than I'm telling her. But as far as I know, she doesn't know about his family's politics. It's not like his brother is a household name—yet.

This isn't where my head should be. I need to be thinking about work, not my personal vendetta, but the fight is in five days and everything is sliding into place. I'm losing my ability to separate the two, and my partners still don't know about Tabitha.

Jason comes in carrying two extra-large pizza boxes. "Is it game time yet?"

"Not funny," Cole mutters, his eyes on the screen. One of the local PRISM principals is his estranged mother-in-law, an heiress with an ambiguous sense of right-and-wrong and a generous purse for destabilizing forces. He expects her to show up tonight, and the fact Spencer Rook is there takes that to a whole different level.

Like his extended family getting tangled up in the America First white supremacy movement.

Amelia Dashford Reid probably isn't racist, but she's probably not anti-racist, either.

How she managed to spawn Hailey is beyond all of us but we're all better for knowing her daughter. Too bad the same cannot be said for Mrs. Dashford Reid herself.

Jason takes the seat next to me. "Everything working as you expect?"

I nod. "We've got good coverage. A couple of visual dark spots, but the audio pick-up is excellent. I love the new microcontrollers I found, they're—"

"Got it. Contain your gadget lust."

"You asked."

"And you answered more than sufficiently. Any sign of anyone else listening in?"

"Nobody's planted anything since I did. I don't know about before that, but you said the rooms were scrubbed yesterday morning?"

"Yeah."

"And nobody else knows about the meeting."

He shakes his head. "I don't think so."

"Well, it's not like it matters. We'll share it through the usual channels if there's anything interesting." There was so much information being poured into the dark web, it would be a miracle if anyone noticed or cared.

Most hackers think Rook is a joke.

But they take PRISM seriously, as they should. If this is in fact a meeting of minds that leads to a new partnership, that will be an explosive bombshell.

It'll give Rook an underground legitimacy he's been craving, and PRISM instant access to an angry network of home-grown vigilantes.

I didn't bother to try and pick up Rook's public conversation taking place downstairs in the bar, but I did leave a camera down there to get a visual. There's a Washington Post reporter five feet away. If he says anything unexpected, it'll be reported.

What is interesting, though, is how large and enthusiastic a crowd a white supremacist can draw in downtown D.C.

Interesting in a haven't-we-learned-anything, no-of-course-not kind of way.

I use our visual recognition software to document those in attendance, then flip the display order around so the biggest screen shot is of the room we expect them to use, and the second biggest space on the screen is for the back alley, where I think they'll arrive.

And sure enough, a black town car pulls up. Out steps a

man in his fifties with a round face and a nothing smile. He looks smooth and carefree, like the ultra-wealthy often do, and I peg him immediately as one of our secret guests.

"Who is that?" Jason leans in.

I zoom and capture a good shot. When we're lucky, the system finds a match right away. This time, nothing comes up. The search is still spooling as I reset the camera and we watch him mount the stairs. "Nothing in the domestic databases. Searching foreign resources next."

"Diplomat, maybe?"

"Probably, if they've been scrubbed from the American lists. I'll get the bots on it, but we probably won't know before the end of the meeting."

"We'll call him Mr. X for now."

The next car has three people in it. Amelia, another anonymous middle-aged man, and an obvious bodyguard. His, I think, as again it's a face that's not immediately traceable.

PRISM was slick, no doubt about it. And they didn't give a fuck about operating in plain sight.

The next hour passes agonizingly slowly. They get settled in the room upstairs and talk about what sounds like nothing. A waiter brings them drinks, and we all wait for the meeting downstairs to break up.

———

Rook stops in the men's room on his way upstairs. Presumably to check his hipster hair cut and fix his ugly fucking tie.

When he's ushered into the room upstairs, he's got a cocky, easy grin on his face. He knows who Amelia is, clearly. He holds out his hand and directs his first comments to her. "Spencer Rook. A pleasure to meet you, ma'am."

"The pleasure is all ours. Please, have a seat. I understand you had a little salon downstairs just now. How did that go?"

"As it always does." He grins and leans back in his chair, smug bastard. "It's a joy to help people get fired up about protecting the white race."

"You've gotten some press with your Institute lately. How do you feel that's helping your cause?"

"No such thing as bad press."

"Even if it invites the scrutiny of the FBI?"

"Law enforcement is overwhelmingly white male. They feel the truth of what I'm saying right here." He taps himself on his chest.

"Who else does your message resonate with?"

"Working men and women. People left behind by trade agreements and technological advances that have replaced their jobs with robots."

"Manufacturing," Mr. X says.

"Definitely. But small business owners, food industry. It's hard to make money in small town America today. We've forgotten our dream because big business, wall street elites, and special snowflakes are in charge." That he could say that straight-faced to three people with a combined wealth greater than a small nation was remarkable.

That they didn't even blink was even more so.

They don't mind his rhetoric.

Hell, maybe it's even what they're looking for.

What else does that rhetoric provide cover for?

It doesn't take long for Amelia to show her hand. "One last question. Who are you supporting for President next year?"

Rook rubs his hands together. "Our base likes Howard Simon." A Republican senator from Florida whose official portrait has him wearing hunting gear. I pull up the dossier as we listen.

That's not going to interest PRISM. He's a two-issue candidate at best who won't make it far in the primaries.

Amelia gives Rook a big smile anyway. "I'll have to make a generous donation to his campaign, in that case." She stands and holds out her hand. "Lovely to meet you, Mr. Rook. We'll have to do this again."

"Spencer, please." He gives her a flirty smile that makes my skin crawl. "And I'd love to meet your family—"

The rest of what he says is drowned out by Cole, who jumps to his feet, arms cocked and neck veins bulging. "Shut your fucking ugly gob, you piece of shit. Jesus Christ, I can't wait to take you down."

It's not funny, but...it's a little funny.

I glance sideways at Tag. He's trying not to smirk, too.

Cole swivels around. "What?"

I shake my head. "Nothing." I get it. He just doesn't know that I get it yet. We'll do anything for our women. And our country, too, although we're all trained to have patience and plan for the right counter-attack on the latter front.

Nobody trained us to be elite forces in the areas of love and emotional attachment.

As Cole throws himself back into his seat, we watch a silent exchange happen between Amelia and her Mr. X compatriot. The third man in the room finally breaks his silence. "Well," he says in a slow, flat accent. Dutch, maybe. I've got voice recognition going, too, but I doubt it'll help identify him. "So this man can be useful to us? How?"

"We think his message could have wide popularity if properly packaged."

"Tell me more."

Amelia smiles, cold and calculating. "We like Victor Best."

I jerk upright, my tablet spilling out of my hands and clattering onto the conference table.

Jason holds up his hand, telling me to keep my mouth shut so we can listen to this conversation.

"He is running as a Democrat, no? Really? And you want to pair me with this little fascist?"

She laughs. Crazy bitch. "Rook isn't a fascist, he's a nationalist. And he's speaking about the fears of people everyone has has written off. Those disenfranchised voters could be exactly what we need to sweep to power. And Victor Best is the candidate to invigorate them. I don't care if he's a liberal or a conservative. He's belonged to both parties. And more to the point, he believes in neither. That's the most useful element to us, after all. Moral flexibility."

Quiet laughter filters over the wires as all three chuckle at that.

"We'll back all horses, of course, to varying degrees. But right now, my money's on Best. He's shaking things up in a way we like."

"And Rook?"

"Let's see what we can do about arranging a meeting between them. It might surprise you how interested Best might be in the idea of appealing to everyday working people. Popularity is his strongest motivator."

"We'll need to install someone we can trust close to him to manage this relationship between them."

"The council is in agreement on that."

"Then make it so. Now, let's talk about the psychometric stuff coming out of England. What Reggie shared was fascinating, but it's a gamble."

"That's my favorite thing," Amelia says. I glance at Cole, who's face is hard as granite and unreadable.

To say he hates his mother-in-law would be putting it mildly.

A grunt comes next over the speakers. Noncommittal.

My fingers fly over my keyboard, tap on my mouse. Its early morning in the UK but my contact in Cambridge is a light sleeper and works odd hours. Either way he's not going to want to miss this.

"Jason," I say quickly. "How much of this can I share with Bryan at Cambridge?"

He shrugs. "It's just political meddling. Damning for people who care, but nothing life changing for the masses. Give him an encrypted link to a raw feed, and he can have it all."

Nobody credible is hunting conspiracies anymore. The crackpots ruined that fun for us, because now there are so many fake conspiracies out there that digging into the real ones doesn't get any traction. Even Anonymous doesn't care about shit like that.

Now we're just watching the world burn and figuring out what the power dynamics will be when we get a chance to rebuild.

Branch, Gough, Nix...even Wilson. Every role I've ever adopted has been built on the premise that this destruction of democracy was a given, and I'd need to be well positioned for when it happened.

For the first time in a long time, I find myself wishing it weren't so.

As the conversation continues, I tune out. It doesn't matter. They'll pull their strings. We'll cut some and tangle others. Some we won't be able to reach, because nothing is as simple as a gladiator roaring at a beast.

I was fifteen when I went to college. Seventeen when I was expelled. When I came to Washington full of fire and ideals, and realized my government only wanted my skills to fuck up the world on their behalf. So a shadowy international organization backing a narcissistic billionaire in his bid for President shouldn't surprise me, and it shouldn't re-awaken that idealistic teenager hacker inside me, but it does on both counts.

I'm still lost in my own thoughts when Tag pauses the video feed, shifting the focus in our conference room to the next question—so now that we know PRISM has a vested interest in the next Presidential election, what do we do about that?

I know what Jason's going to say, and I'm not wrong. "We can't interfere."

"Why the fuck not?" Cole waves his hand at the now frozen image of the PRISM council principals on the screen. "They are."

"Because we're better than them?" Tag drawls, clearly amused at the way the conversation has twisted.

"Is that a question?" Cole growls.

"Some days." Tag shrugs. "Don't get so distracted by the moral outrage that you miss the long game. If we interfere now, we don't hurt PRISM at all. We don't even hurt Best. They pivot and move in a new direction. The only way to actually hobble them is the wait until they're invested. Until they've committed to a plan."

"You're talking about letting them take this all the way to the White House."

"If not him, it'll be someone else. The Republicans are going to nominate Senator Vance, and she's going to lose. So yeah. Maybe Best takes the White House. And that's when we hit him. And if he stumbles in the primaries and doesn't secure the nomination, then Karma will have done her work for us. But we don't play with unintended consequences." He slaps his hand flat on the table. "We all know better than that."

I'm not sure I do.

I clear my throat. "Speaking of unintended consequences..."

[28]

WILSON

"You have got to be fucking kidding me." Jason drops his voice, cold as ice, and paces away from the conference table. Tag and Cole's faces are similarly stony.

Maybe telling them right now wasn't a great idea.

"It was personal." I cross my arms over my chest. "And now that there's a complicating factor that makes part of it not so personal, I shared. Would you rather I have continued to keep silent?"

"You don't think we would have noticed next week when you get arrested in an FBI sting that arrests a major music industry manager and a *candidate for President of the United States of America?*"

"When I put the plan together, he was a fringe candidate."

"Not so fringe anymore."

"I see that."

"You knew that last night," Cole interjected. "When Deacon Webb told you he was being assigned to Best's detail."

"Here's hoping the Secret Service keeps him away from the fight, then."

"And if they don't? This is a convoluted way to get your girlfriend out of a messy relationship. Maybe operations planning isn't your forte."

"You got a better plan?"

"If I came up with one, could you even shift gears?" Jason's yelling by the end of the question. "No, we'll make this work. But you're bringing us in, on everything. Right fucking now."

I take a deep breath. "Easier to show you at my place."

———

Tag lets out a low, long whistle as he looks at the wall in my loft. Around the domino parade of names are a list of bank routing numbers, connected to domain addresses, dates, other names...a complete web of money and masked confusion. "This is old-school vengeance, dude."

I take that as a compliment. "Thank you."

Cole laughs. "Okay, explain it to those of us that don't think in binary."

"For months, I've been waiting for Grant to do something illegal. Hire an underage hooker, gamble on the wrong thing. Jackass hasn't. So I decided I had to do it for him, and with his brother's money to boot. Those are small denomination donations to Rook's so-called charity. They funnel in and then right back out of his company accounts. He does accounting once a month, so he'll notice this at some point, but he'll just find his brother. I don't really care how that plays out. Then the money drops here—" I tap at Grant's name. "And he uses it to bet on the fights. I pushed data packets onto his computer from the last dozen broadcasts, so the feds will find that trace after they arrest him."

"And how they are going to discover him?"

I wince. "This is the part that includes Best, and unfortunately, I've already pulled the trigger. He's also exceeded the personal contribution limit out of the same account, to the tune of ten thousand dollars. Ten thousand dirty, racist dollars that the Best account will be forced to report to the Federal Elections Commission in the next day or two."

"Triggering an investigation into that account?" Jason's jaw is still tight as a steel coil, but there's a grudging admiration in his voice that gives me hope.

"Yeah. Ideally, they're watching him as he bets on the fight, and they swoop in to arrest him at the event."

"You want him there in person?" Cole shakes his head. "Wouldn't it be better if he was arrested at a hotel or something? Reduces the risk of..." He waves at the wall in the middle, where I've listed who I think might be at the fight in Vegas. Including now myself, as Nix. "You going to jail as well."

"Unless he's there in person, it's all circumstantial evidence. And a good hacker would be able to unravel what I've done, or at least show that all the fingerprints were digital only, and therefore questionable. His physical presence greatly reduces the chance they even send the digital stuff beyond their in-house tech guys. The entire case will be about his bets that night, not as much about the validity of the donation money." I let out a long, slow breath. "Or that's the plan, anyway."

"It's good." Jason nods. "We're in."

"No." I shake my head. "I can't ask you guys to do that."

Cole gives me a hard look. "I asked you to take fucking knitting lessons from my woman. We're in. This is what we do. Besides, how are you getting him to go to the fight?"

"That's the most beautiful part of it all. He was already in Vegas that night. Victor Best is going to invite him, and send a car. And he's going to believe it, because he's just that shallow."

"Excellent. I'll be the driver."

"And we'll be your eyes and ears outside the fight," Jason

says. "Worst case scenario, we can run interference with the Feds."

"Worst case scenario is that I end up pummelling the guy to death. He's going to recognize me. If he engages..."

Jason just shrugs. "That would be a bad idea on his part."

No fucking kidding.

[29]

TABITHA

WHEN A STAGEHAND KNOCKS at my dressing room door and asks me if it's a good time for a visitor, I'm expecting him to introduce Victor Best. Instead of the fifty-something billionaire, though, it's his twenty-something wife who steps inside.

"Oh, hi!" I swivel out of my chair and put down the extra-pointy necklace I was just abut to put on in case Victor tried to hug me. "I'm Tabitha."

She laughs and steps closer, holding out her hand. "Ginnifer, nice to meet you. I think, right? We haven't met before?"

I shake my head. "I've met your husband once or twice at things, but I think this is the first time for us. I was expecting him, in fact. My manager said he was in town."

Something passes quickly behind her gaze, then she gives a very practiced smile. "We are. He was." She laughs. "Something came up and he had to fly to Washington unexpectedly."

"Ah, right." He's running for President, although nobody here takes him seriously. "Well, welcome. Are you staying for the show?"

"We are, yes." She points to the hallway. "My step-daughters are big fans of your opening act, so they're meeting them right now. I thought I'd come in and say hello to you."

We couldn't be more opposite, this woman and me. She's wealth and class and sophistication, and I'm...best known for being bisexual.

But she's beaming at me, and I know that look. No, she doesn't want in my pants. That's a similar look. *This* is the look of an adoring fan.

Well how about that. I beam right back at her. "I've got a few minutes, if you want to sit and chat?"

"I'd love that."

It turns out Ginnifer Best is a little bit awkward, and a whole lot nerdy. I know her official back story. She was a teen beauty queen in Florida, and her parents were friends with Victor Best and his previous wife. When his wife fell ill with breast cancer, nineteen-year-old Ginnifer joined the family as an au pair to their two pre-teen daughters.

And when he was widowed two years later, he married his nanny within three months.

Their son, Thomas Jefferson Best, was born eleven months later.

I remember how young and innocent—and overwhelmed—she looked in those early days under constant media scrutiny. Now she's poised and polished on screen, but right now as we talk about the pressures of living out of a suitcase and managing a business from the road—because she has a successful fitness and health website, too—I see glimpses of that innocent girl, thrust into a life she wasn't fully prepared for.

I know all about that.

Hang on for the ride, honey.

"Can I tell you a secret?" she asks, leaning in.

"Of course."

"I used to sing *Fly* to my son when he was a baby. I know it's dark, but...there's something about it that makes it a lullaby. Is that weird?"

Hot, unexpected tears burst behind my eyelids and it takes everything in my power to not let them fall. "No," I whisper. "That's sort of how I wrote it. Nobody's ever picked up on that before."

"Really?" She looks down at her hands and flutters them. "Then they aren't listening closely enough. It's beautiful. Anyway, I should let you finish getting ready, and we need to take our seats..."

I stand, and when she leans in for a hug, I let her. We're both wearing heels, but she's got a solid six inches on me, and my cheek presses into her shoulder.

For a society lady, she gives really good Mom hugs.

I realize with a weird, painful start that I don't actually remember when I had an embrace like this. Shit, I'm totally going to cry on her thousand-dollar silk blend t-shirt.

And I'm still hugging her.

I drop my arms and step back, and we both laugh.

"This is going to sound weird," she starts to say at the same time as I open my mouth.

"What are you guys doing tomorrow?" I ask, thinking I could invite her and her step-daughters to do something age appropriate, since after the show is not a good idea.

She shakes her head. "We're actually flying to Vegas. Victor's going to meet us there for the weekend, but we have two days of girl stuff planned." She bites her lip. "I know we just met, but...do you want to come with us? When is your next show?"

"Monday in Salt Lake City." I give her an incredulous look, because this is kind of serendipitous. "And most of my band and crew are already going to Vegas. I wasn't planning on it, but... plans can change."

We exchange contact information, and she reassures me there's lots of room on their private plane for me to come with them.

Even for a rock star, this is kind of surreal, but okay.

I think I've found my first friend who doesn't want to fuck me, fuck me over, or use me for my music connections. Not at all how tonight was going to go down, but even better.

During the show, I dedicate *Fly* to her, and point into the darkness. Ginnifer Best, the universe is conspiring in the weirdest of ways, but I think I like it.

[30]

WILSON

WASHINGTON

She isn't picking up her phone.

This is my own fucking fault for not paying closer attention to the tapes. For being so distracted by my plans that I forget the most important task of keeping her fucking safe.

And now she's on a plane to Las Vegas.

I glare up at the departures board at Dulles. In another forty-five minutes, so will I, but how the hell do I tell her she needs to leave after that look on her face when Best's wife invited her to have a girls' trip?

Another reason I shouldn't have kept this from my partners. Cole could have introduced Tabitha to Hailey.

Women need that kind of thing.

I was so obsessed with having her all to myself that I missed that basic point. And now she's going to be right in the eye of the storm.

"What is it?" Jason asks as he comes to a stop next to me.

"Are you done buying souvenirs?" I snap.

He laughs. "Sure. On edge, much?"

"Tabitha's going to Vegas."

"When?"

"Right now. She's on Best's private plane with his wife. They're new-found best friends."

"I like his wife. She's hot."

"Not the point."

"I'm a red-blooded man. It's always the point to a certain extent." He makes a dismissive grunt and shrugs his shoulders. "Anyway. So what are you going to do about Tabitha?"

An excellent question.

[31]
TABITHA

The second I let myself into my suite, I know I'm not alone.

I take a deep breath and curl my fingers in, forming a loose fist as I stride into the living room space. "What are you doing here?"

Grant gives me a loose, sneering shrug as he lifts a glass to his mouth. "Catching up. It's been a few days."

"We left Portland this morning."

"But *we* flew on a regular ol' jet plane, and you came with Victor Best's wife." He pins his cold gaze on me. "What's that all about?"

"You said be nice to the man. The man didn't show up, but his wife did, so I was nice to her. Just where exactly did I go wrong this time?"

"You're playing at something."

"You're paranoid." I stop in front of him and kick at his foot. "Get out of my suite. Don't you have something better to do?"

He holds up a piece heavy white card stock. "Maybe. Did you have anything to do with this?"

I reach out my hand to take it, and he holds it just out of reach.

Fine. Whatever. I stalk to the minibar and grab a mineral water.

"It's an invitation from Best to join him for a fight on Saturday night."

I glance back over my shoulder at him. "Ginnifer said he'd be in town by the weekend."

"Are you going?"

"I didn't get the invite."

"She didn't say anything about it?"

I shrug. "No. Maybe it's not a socialite kind of event. Where is it?"

"No address. Just a time, and an instruction to meet a driver out front."

"Fun." I don't bother to hide my sarcasm. A fight sounds awful.

"Work on your enthusiasm. You're coming with me."

"I am not."

"You still need to impress Best."

A tension headache starts to pull at the back of my neck. "The invitation wasn't for me, was it?"

He stands, getting right in my face. "Are you being difficult?"

It would be so easy. Grab his arm behind the elbow, jack my hip up into his. Use my lower center of gravity to my advantage like Wilson taught me.

Knock him onto his back and then step on his nuts.

Instead, I shake my head. "No more than usual. But I've got plans on Saturday night."

"Cancel them."

We have a silent stand-off, glaring at each other, then he pushes past me and storms out.

Swearing under my breath, I stalk after him and slam the security bolt shut, then turn around and scream.

Wilson's standing in front of me, and he's pissed.

"What the hell are you doing here?" I gasp, rubbing my chest for a second before taking halting steps towards him.

He closes the gap and touches his fingertips to my cheek. "I could say the same thing to you."

"Why?" I turn my face into his hand and let my eyelids flutter shut as he brushes his lips over my jaw and onto my neck.

"It's a long story. Shhh." His mouth covers mine, soft and insistent, and oh my God, how I've missed him.

Breathing hard, I press closer, letting his kiss fill the emptiness inside me. I curl my tongue against his when he pushes into my mouth, welcoming his too-long-absent exploration.

How did I push him away? I never want to let him go, ever again. I cling to his broad shoulders as he walks me back into the door, pressing me against the cool wood as he draws his flat palm down the heavy curve of my breast and onto my waist.

"How long have you been in my suite?" I ask as he kisses his way down my neck again.

"Since before he let himself in." He pulls away and gives me a hard look. "Why does he have a key to your room?"

I glare right back. "We've stayed here before, and he usually takes care of all the room bookings. He didn't this time, but I'm assuming he just asked the front desk for a card."

He scrubs a hand quickly over his face. "Are you okay?"

"No. Men keep letting themselves into my hotel suite and scaring the everliving shit out of me."

"Sorry." He doesn't look it, though. He still looks mad. I wish we were still making out.

I reach for him again, lacing my fingers through his. "What is going on? Why are you in Vegas?"

"I told you."

"Long story?" I snort. "I've got time. And this time maybe we can get through it all without kissing."

"Doubtful." He leans in and brushes his lips against mine. "I've missed you."

"I was mean to you."

"Yeah, you were. But I'm a big boy, and I can handle it."

"Is that what this is about? Handling it?"

"Maybe."

"Wilson..."

"Tabitha..." He nips at my lower lip. "I'll tell you everything, but you need to promise not to freak out."

"That's not a good sign." I close my eyes and exhale. "Fine. I promise."

"Grant's been making some bad bets on dangerous, underground fighting, with money that isn't his and that's tied to hate speech. He's going to get nabbed by the FBI for it, and his very well-paid attorney is going to make a deal that will preclude him talking about any of his crimes, including document forging and possible child endangerment. The last two off the record, of course."

My eyes fly open as I try to process that. "He's *what?*"

Wilson waits for me to catch up.

"I... I can't believe it. He's never been a gambler, he's way too..." I shove my hand against Wilson's chest. "Wait a second."

"What?"

"You did that."

"Yeah."

"What the hell are you thinking?" I shove him harder, and he doesn't move. "Is that what that invitation is all about?"

"Maybe."

"You are... insane. This is... insane. I can't even... Why?"

"Because you need him out of your life."

My jaw drops open. "Isn't that my call?"

"Would you ever have made it?"

I stop. Just...dead. No, I would never.

He doesn't blink, and he doesn't move. "You can make it now. You can tell me to back off, and I'll do my best to unravel what I've done. But this is what I do, Tabitha. I make bad people pay for shit."

"Shit they haven't done."

He shrugs. "Minor detail. Would you rather he pay for horrifying domestic violence? Because I would. I want him hung in the public square for what he did to you, but I don't want you to suffer through that. I don't want you to have to talk about Keegan, or the life you left behind, or living on the streets. I want to make him disappear in a way that doesn't touch you. And if that means inventing a financial crime, I'm good with that."

I start to shake as he's talking, and he leans in and wraps his arms around me.

"I'd do anything for you."

"You know when people say that, they don't usually mean it without any limits," I whisper.

"Then they're doing love the wrong way," he whispers back.

A lump catches in my throat.

"Don't go with him to the fight," he grinds out as I lean into him.

I close my eyes. "Will you be there?"

"Don't, Tabitha. It could get really dangerous."

"Is Victor Best really going to be there?"

He hesitates. "No."

"Okay." I take a deep breath. "What can I do?"

"Nothing."

That's not going to fly with me. I try again, this time starting with a reassurance. "I'll stay far away on Saturday night. But in the next two days...what can I do?"

He hesitates, then presses his lips against my temple. "It would help if he was unhinged. Reckless."

I let out a shaky breath. "Unhinged and reckless are my specialities."

[32]

TABITHA

We're at the spa in the hotel, getting pedicures, but it's not exactly relaxing because Ginnifer's phone keeps going off.

Since Victor owns the hotel, the staff don't say anything, but her stepdaughter does.

"You're not supposed to be using that," Clara says, complete with a bored sixteen-year-old eye roll.

"It's your father." Ginnifer chews on her lower lip. "We have to go to Washington tonight."

A weird ribbon of relief curls through my stomach. I know that there was really no chance of her being affected by whatever's going to go down tomorrow night—on the other side of the city, in a warehouse completely removed from this world of luxury—but I don't want her involved.

There's something fragile and innocent about her.

Clara makes a grumpy face, and Ginnifer just waves her off. "Oh, shush. You knew this was coming."

"It's going to be such a *drag* having Secret Service protection."

Ginnifer points at the hulking man standing at the far end of the hall. "We have bodyguards now."

"That's different."

"I'm sure it's not." She sighs as yet another message comes in, and then puts her phone away and glances at me. "Although who knows, right? Whole new world. Sorry to leave you on your own for the weekend."

I lift my toes out of the bubbling water. "I'm going to be just fine."

Clara's phone rings, and she answers it with an exaggerated, "Hello?"

Ginnifer snaps her fingers and points to the door.

Clara gives her a look of disbelief. "You were using yours."

"For texting your father. Out you go. Conversations in the privacy room only. You know the rule."

She waits until Clara's gone to thump her head back against the chair. "Teenagers. It was like, ten minutes ago I was one myself. I'm not cut out for this."

I give her a sympathetic look. "You guys have an interesting relationship."

Her younger step-daughter and her son are in their hotel suite watching a movie with a nanny right now, but Clara wanted to come along with us—and has complained non-stop since.

"She knows I'm on her side, but I'm not her friend, and I'm not her Mom, either. It's weird. But we're figuring it out. Victor..." She trails off and I don't push. None of my business. "Anyway, she's the least happy out of all of us about his campaign. I think that's probably the way it is for most teenagers. Nobody wants to give up their freedom."

"I bet not."

She laughs. "I think about what I was like at fifteen, and I just...yeah. I try to have patience for her. It's a hard age. Right?"

"Right," I murmur. But I don't know, really. I didn't get a chance to be that petulant brat. Or maybe I did, and it's what killed my son. Either way, I can't relate without wanting to throw up, so I pick up the nail polish color beside me and pretend I'm not sure about it after all.

"That's a nice color. I miss bold choices like that."

I hold it out to her. "You want it?"

She shakes her head. "Only variations on nude for me. Victor has particular tastes."

I lift my eyebrow and wiggle it suggestively. "Maybe he'd like a surprise."

She blushes. "Oh, no. Definitely not. And I didn't mean it like that. He doesn't have a nail polish fetish or something."

"Trust me, it would be the most normal fetish I've discussed this week if he did."

Now her face turns bright red, and I realize I've gone too far.

"Sorry," I say, trying to laugh it off. "Just ignore me."

"Let's just say that your songs are the closest I've gotten to sex in a while," she mutters, and before I can react to *that* bombshell, her step-daughter returns.

———

After pedicures, we head back to her suite to have lunch with her kids, and I put Operation Mess-With-Grant's-Head into motion.

Tabitha: I've been thinking about the next leg of the tour. Can we meet?

Grant: The one that starts in four days? No thinking allowed.

I roll my eyes. Like I don't know how to push his buttons. I've been watching and waiting for this for ten years.

Tabitha: So that's a no to meeting? Fine. It'll be a surprise, then.
Grant: Where and when?
Tabitha: Coffee in the lobby cafe in an hour?
Grant: Fine. But don't get excited about anything crazy. No changes are happening.

———

I'm drinking a green tea when he arrives.

"You're late," I say, not quite looking at him.

He takes the seat across from me. "What's going on?"

I take a deep breath and force myself to meet his gaze. I never hold eye contact with him. It hurts too much. For all the success he's helped me achieve, he's also the source of my greatest pain. "I want to make some changes."

"Like what?"

"The fans aren't excited about the concerts. They're the same old thing. I want do something different." I swallow hard. "I want to be something different."

That triggers something inside him.

Good. Be afraid.

I've never cared that much about my image. I've let them craft me into what they want to be, but fuck it. Two more days, and I'll be free to be whoever I want to be.

Maybe I should have done this years ago.

"Don't be rash," he says quietly. "Your fans love you."

"Then why haven't they turned up? We made tickets as cheap as we could make them. Hmm?" I shake my head. "They aren't my fans. Not really. They love what I sing when it's on the charts, because it's easy to consume. Sexy and fun. But once I drop off, poof. They're on to the next hot single. That's not to my benefit. That's maybe to your benefit, if you're looking to find the next hot young thing."

Another flare in his eyes, and *holy shit.*

"Grant?" My voice chills. "Are you looking for another client?"

He doesn't answer me.

"Good luck with that," I say, standing. "Good fucking luck."

He snaps his hand out and circles his fingers around my wrist. "Nobody wants an angry bitch, Tabitha."

He's wrong. Wilson wants an angry bitch. And that's all that matters. "Fuck you, Grant."

"This isn't over."

If everything goes according to plan, I might never see him again, and that would still be too soon. But I don't want the last words between us to be his. I look him straight in the eye. "You were right, by the way. I have been sleeping with him. And only him. For months."

Fighting a shudder of revulsion, I slide my wrist out of his grasp and head for my room.

I don't look back, not even for a second.

[33]

WILSON

By Saturday evening, we have no idea how this is going to go
down.

Jason did a friendly reach out to the local Feds, saying he
was following a lead on behalf of a client, but they were extra
tight-lipped.

That could either mean they're about to make a bust, or they
have no clue what he was talking about and had totally missed
everything I'd fed them.

We've got back up plans. My favorite is the one where I just
smash Grant into the ground, but that doesn't have any long-
term benefits for Tabitha.

Another is a come-to-Jesus confrontation, but that has to be
her call.

No matter what, his hold on her is coming to an end tonight.

I spend Saturday afternoon holding Tabitha while we both
try to take a nap. When we give that up, we order the most
ridiculous things from room service, then I get her set up with
my tablet which has a Tor browser installed so she can watch
the fight remotely.

"Don't bet on anyone else," I say quietly as she pokes around the web interface.

"How much can I bet on you?" She gives me a sideways glance. "Will it take my black Amex card, or is it some kind of special hacker credits only?"

"Don't bet on me, either." I kiss her cheek. "Just watch. And no matter what happens—even if I get arrested—don't freak out."

"Don't get arrested. That sounds like a bad idea."

"I know. I plan to avoid it."

She's quiet for a long stretch. Then, without looking at me, she says, "I'd bet everything on you, though. Just so you know. Every last penny."

I wrap her in my arms and squeeze her tight.

[34]

TABITHA

My room phone rings an hour after Wilson leaves. I ignore it, but after stopping, it starts again, and I cross the room.

"Hello?"

"What the fuck did you do?" Grant snarls in my ear.

Terror slices through me and I gasp, not even able to scream. I drop the phone at the same time as a bang comes at the door, and the phone handset tumbles off the cradle.

Hang up and call 911, a little voice inside my head says, but it's too quiet and I don't move fast enough. I'm frozen in fear, and everything starts to swim in slow motion around me. I jerk my gaze to the door. The security bolt isn't on, and even while I'm still standing there, thinking I should scramble for the phone like a complete fucking nitwit, he's letting himself into the room.

And he's not alone.

It's been years since I've seen his brother Spencer. Not enough time. They're like two angry, hungry wild animals cornering me as their prey, and I'm still grabbing for the phone.

"Put it down."

I swallow hard and do as Grant orders. I try to stand in front of it in case I have another chance to maybe call 911, but that hope doesn't last long.

Spencer grabs my arm hard enough to jerk my shoulder painfully, and spins me around so I'm facing Grant.

He gets right in my face. The skin around his mouth is white, and his eyes have gone a little crazy. "What. Did. You. Do?"

Okay, a lot crazy.

I have two choices here. I could lie, and try and save myself. Or I can be brave.

That's not a trite idea. It's not easy. I'm shaking so hard my teeth are chattering, but I don't blink and I don't look away. "You can't be surprised, Grant."

"You bitch."

"You stole my life," I whisper. "You had to know at some point I'd take an opportunity to return the favor."

"I gave you a career."

"I didn't want that. I wanted him."

Without warning, he backhands me across the face. I'm stunned silent, which maybe was his goal. He's never hit me before.

"Come on," Spencer bites out from behind me. "We don't have much time."

Grant gives me a hard look. "You've got a fight to get to, baby girl. Big, tough man thinks he's going to save you from me. You're going to set him straight."

Cole: En route. He looks…edgy.
Wilson: Acknowledged.

Twenty minutes later, I'm trying not to look for Grant in the crowd of anonymous faces filling the warehouse. After dropping Grant off in his role as a driver, Cole isn't going to come inside—he'll stay outside, with Jason, providing perimeter eyes and ears.

Tag should be in here, too, but he's on my radio frequency, so he could just say something if he wanted to let me know they'd arrived.

So far, radio silence.

Part of me doesn't want to be distracted. I'm last up for the fights tonight—and if the Feds bust us up before that, I won't be disappointed—but I take the bouts seriously and just in case Nix is going into the ring, he'll come out with his undefeated record intact.

I do a quick check of my phone, and Grant just placed his first bet. Except that was my my bot, as scheduled. It tells me nothing.

I should have tried to get Tabitha to put a GPS tracker on him.

Shoulda, woulda, coulda. No place in a plan for any of that.

I type in her number to check in, but before I hit call, I see him. I slide the phone back into my pocket and start to track him.

He does look edgy, and he's searching the room quite deliberately.

My pulse picks up. He's not confused or overwhelmed by the scene. Damn it. His gaze shifts closer, and I tense.

I see it, the moment he recognizes me. His pace slows, his jaw sets.

I'm not pretending this is a coincidence. Fuck it all to hell.

On the far side of the crowd, I make eye contact with Tag. He gives an imperceptible nod.

Grant stops ten feet from me. We're on the outer edge of the circle of people, but they're all facing the ring.

Nobody is really paying us any attention—yet.

"Whatever you were planning tonight, it's not going to work," he says, raising his voice enough for me to hear him over the din.

Shit. Shit, shit, shit. "Bold statement if you aren't sure what I've got planned. I'm just here to fight."

"Lies!" He screams it at me, wide-eyed and unhinged. "You think you're saving her. She's not worth saving. Joke's on you."

I growl and step closer to him. "Watch what you fucking say about her. I wouldn't hesitate to kill you."

He laughs. "Too late. What's the point? She's already gone."

Blood rushes to my head. "What did you do?"

"Me?" He shrugged. "Nothing. My brother, on the other hand, noticed some suspicious monetary transactions yesterday. Called me about it. Gave me shit. Thanks for that, motherfucker. I had no idea what he was talking about. So he flew down."

"He didn't." My heart is pounding. We were watching Rook. He didn't go anywhere.

"He flew himself." Fuck, the look of pride on Grant's face disgusts me. And the thing is, it's justified. They've bested me.

"He's got Tabitha?" I swallow my anger, my rage, and I force it down, hard, until it's a hard, cold pack of computational fuel. I need data and I need it fast.

"Picked her up from the hotel just before you sent your buffoon to get me. They're watching together now, but not for long."

Sick, cold fear slides into my stomach. "And where did he take her?"

He laughs. "You'll never find out."

Then he pulls out a gun.

Whoa. Rule number one of this very real fight club is no guns. Like the Red Sea, the crowd that hadn't been paying us any attention parts around us. Nobody runs, nobody panics, but the mood is very tense and the focus is now entirely on us.

I can use that.

Fuck.

You don't bring a knife to a gun fight. Or fists. Usually not a good plan. But they're all I have. That and my brain. *Think, asshole.*

I let out my breath, then inhale again, slowly stepping to the left. Moving both of us, because he's following me in the circle, so he's not pointing his weapon at anyone other than me.

And I'm closing the gap a bit, too. Just enough he won't notice. "This is a bad idea, Grant. You don't want to do this here. Lots of witnesses."

"Nobody here will stick around to speak to the cops."

"You sure about that? That's not a smart bet to make, and

you're a smart guy. Look," I hold up my hands, palms out. Little closer. "This is just a disagreement. Nothing to see here. Let's go outside."

His eyes dart to the door, but he doesn't want to move. Why not? Outside would be a better place to shoot me. The second he pulls that trigger, he's going down, he's gotta know that. Outside he has a chance to run.

My brain spins, trying to see this space, this situation, from his perspective. Where did he come in from? Not the door behind me. The far end of the warehouse. The parking lot of the building next door.

That's where he plans to run, when everyone is stampeding out this exit.

He'll never make it. Idiot.

I need more from him. "How about we call your brother? I'll explain to him that this was all on me. I'll explain that to the police, too. We'll straighten this out for him, and for you, and the only person who will take any kind of fall will be me."

His shoulder pulls up when I mention the cops. Okay, I won't do that again. But he's frowning, too, like he's not sure what to do. Poor planning, guys, if it's this easy to create confusion.

And again, he's reluctant to be moved away from the line-of-sight of the far exit. He doesn't go as far as to look in that direction, but there's a strong draw there.

What could be over there, specifically? Then it clicks.

His brother.

My woman.

Okay. I need to test that, then I need to take him out. But I don't have a lot of time. He's getting tense, and the acrid stink of fear is rolling off him now.

"The only thing that matters to me," I say softly, "is making sure that Tabitha isn't hurt."

Flinch.

"Is that what he's going to do? You can stop him. You've never hurt her in ten years. You've been cruel and unkind, but you've never physically laid a hand on her. I see you. I see how you've protected her in your own way." Fucking hell, that's hard to say.

I've never struggled to lie in a situation like this before.

The truth has never been so important to me.

"You're angry with her."

"She ruined everything."

"She didn't understand," I say softly. Closer again.

He gives me a tortured look. "She told you about the bastard kid."

"Your child." Does he care?

A sneer. "Maybe."

No, he doesn't. Damn. I clench my fists at my side.

"We were never going to let her have the kid. If she didn't have such a good voice, we would have just gotten rid of her completely."

I was never directly involved in interrogation, but I know some of the basics. I know why people suddenly admit to crimes they haven't been accused of, boasting even. Why they ramp up the bravado.

He's getting to the end of his limit.

Well, motherfucker, so am I.

He sees the rage in my eyes. I know he does. He gets this smug fucking look on his face, like, ha, he's hurt me.

He has no idea what pain is.

"Ten years too late," he spits out. "But we're going get the job down now—"

I explode into the air, spinning my body to the side in a three-hundred and sixty degree sideways turn that's hard for him to track with the gun. As I come out of it, he's directly in my path, and my boot connects with his face.

The gun goes off, and I hear the discharge, the zing of a bullet, a crack against concrete.

People are moving now.

I fall on top of him, my fists flying, and I smash him into the ground. Blood slicks my fists as bone and skin give way.

Hands grapple against my arms, trying to get a purchase on me.

"Not yet," I growl. I said I'd kill him and I meant it.

"Carter, leave him." Tag hauls me off Grant's prone body and shoves me toward the door. "We need to get out of here."

"No." I shrug him off and twist, looking for the Glock he had. It had skittered across the floor, and I sweep it up, taking off at a sprint in the other direction.

Footsteps follow, but I don't look back to see who's with me.

There are two sets of steel doors between us and outside. They slam open, ka-bang, ka-bang, and I'm out into the night before either set slams shut again.

I spin in a circle, getting my bearings. We're at the end of a row of warehouses, around back where the loading docks are.

It's cold and dark and quiet.

Tick.

Where are you, Spencer Rook?

Tock.

In the distance, there's a siren. Another. We don't have much time.

An annoying prickle of concern scratches at me. Something is out of place and until I sort through my mental catalog of my surroundings, that heightened sense of impending doom won't settle down.

I don't want it to.

I trust that instinct more than anything else.

Something isn't right, but it doesn't matter.

If this goes sideways, it'll be after I get to Tabitha or die trying.

I'd walk into Hell to stand between her and Lucifer himself.

I see a flash of light a second before I hear the shot snap through the air and hit the wall a few feet from me. "Sniper!" I yell, sprinting ahead. Into Hell indeed.

"Seen," Tag's voice snaps in my ear, over our radios. "Southwest corner of the warehouse."

No, that's wrong. "Southeast," I correct. "Flash was definitely from the front of the warehouse. Repeat. Southeast."

"I have a visual on the southwest roof. Prone sniper."

"Maybe there's two of them." Fuck, fuck, fuck. The door in front of me is locked, but the window's glass. I turn my face away and slam my elbow though it, busting the shards as wide as I can so I can twist my hand and flip the lock. "Jason, you copy? The Feds need to know this is an active sniper situation. They'll want to kill federal agents. This is a setup, and maybe not just for us."

I'm in the building now, and there's a staircase. I take the stairs two at a time. I've got Grant's Glock, and I check the magazine. Maybe twenty rounds. Time to start counting bullets.

[36]

WILSON

ONE SNIPER MIGHT BE DIRECTLY above me, in the southwest corner. The flash of light I saw was at the other end of the roof, so they've got at least two corners covered. Maybe there are four of them, and they plan to try and hold the building by picking people off, but then why not have an entire militia of crazy psychos to keep me from getting in in the first place?

The stairwell rises up onto the roof, the doorway in a small jut-out in the sky. I turn the handle, then swing the door wide, inviting shots first before I roll out, covering the entire arc of visible space with my weapon as I pivot on my back.

No shots come, but directly in front of me, I see a body with a rifle—and I hear whimpering.

Dread slams into me.

"Hold your fire," I hiss into the comms. "Hold your goddamn fire."

"Report," Jason says back, far too calm.

I can't report. Not fucking yet. I spin around, checking out the far corner of the roof.

I see Spencer now, but he's hunched down behind his rifle and the wind is quite loud up here. He may not have heard the door open, as it was facing away from him behind that jut-out. I grab it before it can swing shut, and silently put it back in place.

"Visual confirmation. Southeast corner, Spencer Rook with a sniper rifle. Southwest corner—" My voice cracks. "His hostage, bound and placed next to a rifle. He wants her shot dead. She may be injured. I need cover."

"Ninety more seconds and you'll have it, the Feds are moving into position."

A minute and a half.

I tell myself to take the time to deal with my hands and elbow, all bleeding. To catch my breath and force myself into a place of calm discipline.

It doesn't work. I spend every second until that megaphone crackles to life below freaking the fuck out about whether or not she's injured already.

As soon as the FBI spokesman starts talking to Rook, I'm in motion, running lightly across the roof and sliding into place next to Tabitha. I work on the ropes first, untying the knots and rubbing circulation back into her hands.

She reaches for me, clinging to me even as she sobs quietly.

"Listen. Listen to me." I grip her chin. "I'm going to get you out of here. But you need to do something for me, okay?"

She nods jerkily and I kiss her forehead. "You need to stop crying now. You need to be a quiet little church mouse, and the next time the guy with the megaphone is talking, you need to run to that door right there and race down the stairs as fast as you can. Someone will take you from there. I'm going to stay here in your place, so if he looks over here, he thinks you're still where he put you."

"No, come with me," she whispers.

"I can't let him start shooting at the cops down there." I kiss her forehead again. "Ready?"

"No."

"Wrong answer." The megaphone crackles to life again, and I haul her up, practically throwing her in the direction of where I just came from.

She spins and scrambles, then freezes at the door.

I force myself to keep breathing. She needs to get the hell off this rooftop. If I take a shot at Rook, he's going to shoot back, and the walls around that stairwell won't protect her. She's safe from his eyes, but not his gun.

Unless I don't miss.

Better not fucking miss, then.

Don't gamble with her safety, asshole. No, I've done enough of that for a lifetime already.

In my ear, Jason clears his throat. "They're settling in here for a long hostage situation. That feel accurate to you?"

I press my mic and lower my voice. "Doesn't need to be. If I get a clear shot, should I take it?"

A long pause. "Yes."

I swivel my head back to where Tabitha's standing, still frozen, at the door. In the moonlight, she holds my gaze. I try to tell her wordlessly that I know she can do this, that she has to, that it'll be okay. I don't know if she gets any of that, but with a strangled cry, she turns and pulls the door open, disappearing inside.

Exhaling, I tap the mic again. "Tabitha's coming down. Alone."

"We'll get her." I don't hear anything, and there's no commotion in the alley below, but after a few seconds, there's another radio crackle in my ear.

This time it's Cole. "Got her. Far side of the building. Sheltering in place until SWAT can cover us."

Excellent.

My pulse jumps in relief, cold sweat breaking over my back.

Now to take out this guy before he kills anyone.

People think you can shoot to injure someone, to incapacitate them in a way that still makes it neat and tidy for the cops to make an arrest. That's not how it works. You always shoot to kill. Center of mass, good. Head shot, great. Turn out the lights. Bam.

But sometimes you miss, and you get their arm, a leg.

I'm a good shot, but at this distance, with the wind and the darkness, I'll be lucky to hit whatever I can.

Oh, Spencer Rook. A week ago, you were a breath away from helping play a role in shaping the next President of the United States of America.

And now you're about to eat my bullet. I brace myself against the wall and aim.

Snap.

He drops his rifle with a howl, and I take another shot. His shoulder this time. Suddenly the roof explodes with activity, SWAT pouring out of both staircases, and I hold my hands in the air, Grant's pistol tumbling to the ground.

Good enough.

———

I'm handcuffed and marched downstairs, but our story of investigating Grant on Tabitha's behalf flies well enough with the Feds that I'm released before we even get out of the warehouse.

When we step outside, they're loading Grant into an unmarked car. Huh. Apparently I didn't kill him after all, although the side of his face looks like my fists did a good number on him.

Not fucking sorry.

He says something which I don't catch, and with a hiss, Tabitha launches herself out of my arms. I don't even try to stop her. Her outstretched hand connects to his face, somewhere between a slap and a gouging scratch, before he's shoved the rest of the way into the car.

Shame it wasn't Cole holding him instead of an FBI agent. We aren't above holding a man down so the woman he's injured grievously can take out her vengeance on him.

I still believe more than most that violence has its place.

There's darkness in this world, and it doesn't respond to polite requests or even cold edicts. It must be brought to its knees by the fist, the hiss, and a solid knee to the groin.

Although the legal system has its place, too.

She's shaking and crying again when she folds into my arms. I suddenly realize it's freezing, and I try to cover as much of her body with mine as I can.

"I'm so sorry," I whisper into her hair.

She hiccups into my chest. "You wanted me to come and see you fight."

"Not tonight. Not ever. Not like this."

"You were fighting for me."

"Nothing pretty about it..."

"No." She drags in a ragged breath, then sniffles again. "I guess not."

I clutch her to me, then raise my head, searching for my guys. Cole is right there. "Go on," he says. "Get out of here. Tag will drive you wherever you want to go."

AT SOME POINT after we get in the car, I realize Wilson's covered in blood. Some dry, but not all. There's some fresh oozing on his middle finger that makes my stomach twist. He's holding me tight to his left side, and when I reach across and touch his right hand, he winces.

I jerk my attention to his face. "We need to get you to a hospital."

"I promise I'm fine. I need a shower and a mouthful of pills, that's all."

"You're hurt." I touch his swollen knuckles.

"You're not the only one who got in a hit or two on Grant tonight." He groans. "But the glass in my elbow is more of a problem."

"Glass!" I turn to the guy driving the car and tap on his seat. "He needs to see a doctor."

Wilson tugs me back into his side. "Tag will check out the cuts and stitch me up at the hotel if I need that."

That sounds like something I'm going to have to protest again.

I'm also not sure how we're going to get up to his room

covered in blood, without attracting any attention.

Apparently I'm underestimating how normal this is for these guys. Tag parks underground and hops out. When he opens my door, he's got a way-too-big-for-me parka in his hands. "Slide this on," he says, gently helping me out, and my arms into the coat. "I'll zip it up. There you go."

I'm shaking pretty hard now.

This must be shock setting in.

He leads me around the car and repeats the same effort with Wilson, although his treatment is less kid-gloves, more you're-paying-for-this-coat-you-bleeding-jerk.

The whole time, they're grinning at each other.

No shock there.

The coats might be unusual for Vegas, but maybe we're recent arrivals from North Dakota. And they work—nobody gives us a second look as we head upstairs.

We go to Wilson's room, and Tag heads up to my suite to get my stuff.

"What's going to happen?" I ask Wilson as I help him out of his coat, and then remove my own.

He winces as he checks himself out on the bathroom mirror. "Depends what kind of a case they have on Spencer. They'll both be charged with kidnapping. There might be some organized crime charges as well."

"And the stuff you set up?"

He shrugs. "Most of it will fall away. They don't care about illegal gambling when there are bigger charges to lay."

From the hallway, the click of the lock sounds, and I jump.

He shoots me a worried look. "It's just Tag."

I nod. Gonna be a while before I can hear that sound again.

He raises his voice as his colleague moves my stuff in. "Tag, I could use a pair of scissors in here. And tweezers."

"Got the whole med kit for you." Tag appears in the doorway.

Two big guys and a lot of blood. The bathroom is suddenly very small. "I'm going to lie down on the bed," I say weakly, and Wilson moves to follow me. "I'm fine. Just...let him doctor you up."

I stretch out on the bed and let my head swim as I listen to them talk about steri strips and antibiotic ointment versus stitches.

"Let me see the rest of you," Tag says, and Wilson laughs.

"Get the fuck out. I'm fine. Tabitha can help me."

"I'm not sure she's in any shape to do anything," his partner says.

I scowl. Screw that. I push off the bed and peel off my own torn shirt before stopping in the bathroom doorway. "I heard my name?"

Tag does a double-take at my tits.

I roll my eyes. "Whatever. Jason's seen the entire thing. Ask him about my tattoo."

"Don't ask him about anything," Wilson says, pulling me in as he shoves Tag out. He's half-naked, and he looks like Bjorn Ironside, the kid on Vikings who grew up between seasons two and three in a serious way. Bloodied and muscled and perfect, his baby face all fierce and possessive. "What?"

"You look like the guy on Vikings," I say with a small smile.

"Ragnar?"

As the bathroom door closes, I hear Tag laughing. "Pretty sure she means the blond kid, but sure, Ragnar!"

I lean in and whisper, "The blond kid is super hot."

He shakes his head. "Okay."

"Not as hot as you...Right. Focus, Tabitha. You called for a shield maiden to help you bathe?"

He grins. "I sure did."

I lower myself to his feet and reach for his boots. Pausing before I start on his laces, I glance up at him. "Feels a bit like reverse deja vu here."

"Yeah?"

"You bathed me once."

"That was an excuse to get dirty."

"What do you think this is?" I tease him, but my voice cracks.

He doesn't grin, doesn't bat it away. "It can be whatever you want."

No. That would be... "Let's just get you cleaned up."

I focus on his boots, then I start the shower. When I turn around, he's got his jeans low on his hips, and my mouth goes dry.

He's hard.

He's sliced up, and his hands are battered, and we've just been though a nightmare, and he's hard for me.

"Take off your clothes," he growls, and I do as he commands.

We're broken and scared and dirty. Maybe I'm the only one who's scared. But we're both definitely broken, irrevocably, and fuck it, this is how we deal.

I grab a washcloth and the body wash, as well as the conditioner, before joining him in the small tub, under the small but strong stream of hot water. It's perfect.

"I think you told me to hold still," I whisper as I carefully balance the two containers on the soap ledge.

"I can do that." He braces himself against the tile wall and closes his eyes. I wet the washcloth under the hot water and press it against his face. It streaks rusty red immediately. I rinse it and repeat, over and over again, until the dried blood is gone, and the water swirling at our feet is clear.

Then I lather up some body wash and smooth it over his

neck, his shoulders. Down his chest, and carefully over his hands.

"We should get some ice on these," I whisper, brushing my lips across his knuckles.

"Soon. Heat first." He turns me into the water, running his hands over my body. He cups my breasts, my waist, my hips, then drops to his knees and presses his face to my belly. His lips brush my tattoo, and he shudders. "Tabitha..."

Fuck. I tip my head back, urging the tears to go away, but it's no good. I squeeze my eyes shut as he kisses my cleft, his tongue sliding between my lips and around my clit.

"Let me love you," he groans, sliding my leg up onto his shoulder. "Let me show you..."

He latches on, his tongue flat and his suck strong as he covers my pussy with his mouth. Oh, Lord. *Yes.* "Fuck..."

It doesn't take long for the flutter and thrust of his tongue to get me off, and he keeps licking me until I beg him to stop. I fist my hand in his hair and tug his head back from my very happy cunt. "That was not the plan."

He grins up at me. "But you taste good."

"Stand up." I bite my lip as he obliges, towering over me. I reach for the conditioner. "Now, to get us back on track..."

I slick him up, cock and balls and further still, and he holds at attention for me, letting me touch him wherever I want.

I want everything.

He groans as I stroke him. I twist my hand as I deftly get him off. "Are going to come for me?"

"Always."

"I love watching you," I whisper. "The way your face changes. Sometimes I think it's the only time I see your real face."

"Maybe it is. But—"

"It's okay." I move close, rubbing the wet head of his cock

against my belly. "Come for me. Show me that face. Let me see you."

"You see me." He grunts as I tighten my fingers.

"I do."

"God, Tabitha!" He spurts against fingers, my skin, the shower wall. He shakes, but he holds himself up, and his face twists in passion. Yes. I love that.

And I love him.

Once we're dry, he talks me through fixing his steri strips, then we crawl into bed.

He pulls me close. "We're going to be okay. I'll keep you safe."

How do I make him understand? "Nobody can do that."

"Exactly. I'm nobody. I'm a ghost. I know how to disappear."

"I'm not disappearing." I sound more confident than I feel, but I know this is the right call.

"But..."

"No." I kiss him on the mouth. "I love you, you insane man, and you can give me all the security you want. But I'm not running. I'm going to wake up in the morning and figure out what to do next, but it's not going to be hiding, that's for sure."

"You love me?"

"Of course I do."

"I'm not sure I deserve that, but I'll take it." He tangles his fingers in my hair. "I'll grab it with both hands and hang on tight, because I love you, too. I love you so much I'm afraid I'm not going to be any good at keeping you safe, because I can't think straight."

"I've got you in a tizzy?"

"You do." He laughs. "You so fucking do."

"Well, at least the feeling is mutual."

WILSON

THE NEXT MORNING brings an unexpected calm.

Jason and Cole worked magic overnight, spinning a story of politics and business that was both believable and banal. It made the west coast news, but didn't headline nationally, and Tabitha was kept out of it with the help of an emergency injunction protecting her name in the court proceedings.

We get a visit from the FBI, and later in the day, from the regional Secret Service director. She wanted to know more about Tabitha's new relationship with Ginnifer Best. Had Grant or Spencer said anything to her about the candidate's wife? No and no, and then that was it.

It was all a bit too tidy.

Too neat.

It bothered at me, and when she fell asleep Sunday night, I stayed up and I did some digging.

I haven't looked at her digital footprint in months. It had started to feel weird, and that's saying something for me, because I don't normally have that kind of filter.

But something that had come up in the past is flickering in

my memory. A little flag that whispers, *look over here*. Now I just need to find it again.

I start at her Social Security Number. Newly created when she was fifteen years old.

What would be the justification for that?

What would be legit cover that her identity didn't twig anything at the federal level overnight?

Over the age of twelve, any SSN applications need to be made in person. I glance at the bed, where she's curled up in a ball, her red hair spread across the pillow. Small and innocent.

My eyes scan over the list of acceptable documents. **Certified copy of medical record.**

Then I go back to her SSN. Issued in the State of Washington.

I frown. But Grant's stolen identity was from California.

He'd said this was their plan all along for her...maybe she hadn't had a SSN before. Maybe, name excluded, this was for all intents and purposes a legitimate first SSN. And they'd gotten a doctor to participate in their scheme for reasons that made sense in the fucked up way that sometimes reasons do.

I'd seen stranger things.

I log in to her doctor's website, and from the admin panel, navigate to the supposedly secure side where the health records are kept.

Her last appointment had been for a B-12 shot. It looks like she gets them quarterly. Before that was another B-12 shot and the blood panel we both got in the summer. I hadn't looked at the actual results, though, just the screen shot she'd sent me of the patient note confirming she didn't have any communicable illnesses.

I click in to it now and give a quick scan, but I'm not a doctor.

I go back further, and everything looks ordinary for the

previous year, but two years ago, her doctor flew from Seattle to Tokyo to give her a B-12 shot.

That seems extreme. I've given myself a B-12 shot before. It's not that bad, just a quick jab in the ass.

I frown as I keep scrolling back. Another regular physical, another blood panel. She's been healthy for most of her adult life, and I can't find the start of her B-12 supplementing before I run out of digital health records.

Leaning back in my chair, I frown and run my hand through my hair.

"What is it?"

I glance over at the bed and find her sitting up, holding the sheet in front of her naked body. I give her a half-smile. That's all I can muster right now. "Something doesn't add up, and I'm not sure what it is."

"About what?"

"Your identity."

"You're still worried about that?" She frowns. "Why?"

"I don't know."

"What does the internet say about me?" She climbs out of bed, wrapping the sheet around her, and comes over. I pull her onto my lap and point to the screen. "How long have you been seeing this doctor?"

"Are those my medical records?" She gives me a big, wide-eyed glare. "Wilson!"

"Sorry?"

"Work on that. You should be." She sighs. "Since forever. He was the doctor I saw after I was discharged from the hospital when Keegan died."

"But that happened in Los Angeles."

She nodded. "We flew up to Seattle. I don't remember why."

I open a new window and run a couple of searches on the

good doctor. "Because he's a family friend of the Rooks, it seems."

"He's never said anything about that. I didn't even know that Grant knew him beyond seeing him from time to time at my appointments."

An ugly thought begins to form in my mind. "Tell me about the B-12 shots that you get. Why do you get them at the doctor's office? A nurse or even yourself could administer them at home."

She made a face. "I know, but I'm really needle phobic. And two of them every three months...Easy enough to visit the doctor's office."

"Two needles?" I flip back to her records. "You get a single dose of B-12. That would just be one needle."

She shakes her head. "Two, every time. Jab jab."

My grip on her hip tightens. "I think we need to get some bloodwork done on you when we fly to Salt Lake City tomorrow."

Dirty Love

part five

dirty love

SALT LAKE CITY

When Tabitha gets to The Complex, where her concert will be that night, the first thing she does is have a cast and crew meeting for everyone on her tour. She acknowledges the rumors and tells them that Grant has been arrested and won't be around for the rest of the tour. She encourages everyone to reach out to an anonymous crisis support line if they want to talk about it, but asks them not to speak to the press because of the unexpected news about his estranged family connections.

The second thing she does is put up with a blood draw to humor me. We've hired a well-vetted OB/GYN who runs a fertility clinic here in the city, and he comes with a med lab tech in tow who takes her blood. The doc promises to return after the show, then disappears, and it's almost back to normal.

Except this has never been my normal with her. I roam her dressing room as she gets ready. I've seen this how many times though the distorted lens of a security camera? The way her crew set it up the same everywhere. Cases stacked in exact order, everything labeled.

I glance at her in the mirror. Her eyes are closed and she's running through new lyrics to a song. Same song, just revised again. It's one of the ones they recorded last summer, the one she had a meltdown over.

Her hair stylist smooths one more strand of hair flat, then steps back. "You're good to go, gorgeous."

Tabitha blows her a kiss in the mirror, and then we're alone.

She gives me a look in the mirror, and I move closer. "What is it?"

She shakes her head. "I don't know. I feel like everything has shifted. Like this isn't real."

Grant did this to her. He fucked with her reality in little but concrete ways. I hope he's currently being gang-raped in a Nevada jail. "What do you want this to be?"

Her lips tighten. "I want this to still be real. I want this to not fall apart like a house of cards now." She sucks in a shaky, deep breath. "Wow. I didn't realize any of that. But yeah, very much...that."

"Okay. I was going to ask how much you wanted me to unravel your new identity and weave it back into your old identity, but that answers that question." I squeeze her shoulders.

She shakes her head. "This is me. This is the only name I've ever wanted, and maybe he got it for me, but he didn't *give* it to me. I won't imbue it with that power, or let him take it away from me." She twists in her chair, so she's facing me, then slowly climbs up onto it, kneeling.

She takes my breath away, she's so fucking sexy. Every nerve ending under my skin jumps to life as she wraps her arms around my neck and pulls me in for a soft, sultry kiss. "Thank you," she whispers.

"That's what I'm here for." I push into her mouth with my tongue, deepening the kiss. Fuck, I'm hungry for her. Now is not the time, but she makes me crazy. One slide of her tongue against mine and my brain is buzzing, blocking out reason and work and everything else, because she's my woman and I want to take her.

When we ease apart, I'm hard and she's blushing. She cups my erection through my jeans. "We'll have to take care of this after the show. I do love fucking after a show. I'm going to love it with you even more so."

I bite her, gently. "Good. No more doubts about who you are, okay?"

She shakes her head. "None." She holds out her hand. "Tabitha Leyton. Nice to meet you."

I take her fingers in mine and let her give me a firm handshake. "Wilson Carter. The pleasure is all mine."

"What do you do, Wilson?"

"Crisis management. Out of Washington, D.C. How about yourself?"

She smiles, a brilliant, carefree beam. "I'm a singer. Currently on tour, actually. I need to be in Denver tomorrow."

Is that all? Anything else? I want to ask. But I don't want to steal that light in her eye. Who we are to each other and how we handle that can be a problem for another day. "It just so happens that I'm going that way myself. I'll see that you get there safely."

FOR THE FIRST time this tour, our show is electric. There's this energy that snaps in an amazing show. Songs slide together smoothly, transitions carry the crowd with them, you don't lose anyone.

And when you get to the end of a song, the stadium roars.

It's deafening.

It's my favorite sound in the universe.

There's probably some good psychology there, why I like to be drowned out, but I don't give a fuck tonight.

I'm on fire.

When I get to *Wicked Line*, I'm excited to share the new lyrics. This is version three-point-oh on this song, and frankly, maybe nobody else but me will care about the changes I've made.

Maybe I'm the only one that needs to care about them.

I march right to center stage and stick my mic on the stand. For this one, I want my hands free. I want to shake them in warning and wave them in praise. I want to dance with my people as I weave them a cautionary tale...with a happy fucking ending.

I can't give them the preamble that I want. I can't stand here in front of thousands of people and say, *I'm finally free.* Not yet. But I can sing it.

And I do.

Took a chance on a wicked line
Slick smile, knowing eyes
Was talked into heaven
By a pack of lies

Tumble
Stumble
Get back up
Gimme
Grab me
Flash a smile
Takeaway lesson
Nobody cares

Took a chance on a wicked line
Fast talker, grubby hound
But his dirty secrets
Couldn't keep me bound

The band is going nuts on the last refrain, so I give them the signal we should repeat that, and I do it bluesy this time, slow and proud and dirty.

Mostly proud.

And when we finally stop, and the crowd settles down, I catch my breath in front of the mic stand and I look into the darkness. "Nothing wrong with a little pride, Salt Lake City. Am I right?"

They burn down the house, because I'm totally right.

My high only lasts until the end of the concert. I fly off the stage after the encore and into Wilson's arms, but instead of sex somewhere indecent, he whispers in my ear that the OB/GYN is back and waiting in my dressing room.

I decide not to make an inappropriate threesome joke because the look on his face is serious.

"Ms. Leyton..." He glances past me to Wilson. "Could we have a moment alone? Just one moment, and then if you'd like Mr. Carter to come back in, of course that's perfectly fine."

Wilson waves his hand and ducks out before I can say anything.

I puff out my cheeks and stalk past the good doctor. "Close your eyes for second."

He does, and I pull off my sweat-soaked tank top and grab a dry t-shirt to replace it with.

"Okay, shoot."

"First of all, I've had a chance to review your medical records, and there were some irregularities in your previous care. I asked your...Mr. Carter to step outside because what we discuss only needs to be between us, and it looks like most communication in the past included your manager, a Grant Derew."

"Yeah." I press my hand to my forehead. "That wasn't the smartest move on my part. It's a long, complicated story."

"And I might not be the best physician to get into all of that with, as you don't live here in Salt Lake City, but I take my job seriously and if I can be an ally in any way to you..."

"What's going on?" I cross my arms and look him in the eye. "I've had a crazy past week in ways I can't even begin to explain. Give it to me straight."

"Mr. Carter requested, on your behalf, that we test you for

birth control medication. Synthetic progestin or progesterone, specifically."

All the blood drains from my head. "He did what?"

"The blood work we took earlier. Were you not aware?"

There's a ringing in my ears. I slowly shake my head. "No. That was...I was getting B-12 shots. I thought there was a problem with those. Double the dose or something."

"Ms. Leyton, I don't know how to tell you this, but I think you've been on Depo-Provera most of your adult life."

"I don't understand. I can't...there's no need..."

"There is nothing in your medical history that would suggest you have any kind of infertility."

"I had a baby when I was fifteen," I whisper. "I had a bad c-section. I was told I wouldn't be able to have any more children."

"I don't want to say one way or the other, but there is no reason for you to be getting quarterly shots of progestin other than to prevent a pregnancy."

I point to the door. "Can you...?"

He nods, and the next thing I know, Wilson is in front of me. He stands there like he's not sure if he can hug me, and I burst into tears.

"I'm sorry," he says. "Fuck, I'm saying that a lot."

"It's not your fault," I say, hauling him closer. "How long have you known?"

"Just since last night. And I'm not a doctor, so I thought... I'm sorry."

"Fucking hell. Why would he do that to me?" I mean the doctor, and I mean Grant. I mean them all, the sick, twisted fucks.

Wilson curves his hand over the top of my head, ever so gently, and kisses my forehead. "So you couldn't have more children. So they could control you."

And punish me. Fuck with my head.

Children.

I could have kids. "Wilson..."

———

The next thing I know, I'm lying flat on my back on the couch, and the doctor is kneeling beside me, taking my pulse.

"There she is. Welcome back, Tabitha."

"Did I just faint?" I ask groggily.

Wilson's face blurs into my line of sight. "Like a champ."

I close my eyes and sigh. "Great."

"This was a lot of information to process." The doctor pats my hand. "What time do you move on to Denver tomorrow?"

"The bus leaves first thing."

He hands me his card. "Then let's follow up by phone, and I can recommend someone to do further testing when you get home to..."

"Seattle." My stomach twists. "Not my regular doctor."

The OB shares a dark look with Wilson, then squeezes my hand again. "No. Not that doctor. He's not going to be treating anyone much longer."

Once he leaves, Wilson carefully lifts me off the couch and I curl into his chest.

"So much for it being over," I say quietly.

"How are you feeling?"

"Like I was run over by an emotionally manipulative, gaslighting Mack truck."

He nods above my head. "Right. Stupid question. Let me try again. What can I do?"

I wriggle off his lap and hold out my hand. "Come wash my hair?"

There's a big shower off this dressing room. It's cold and

sterile, every surface tiled, and once the water hisses to life, the splashing drops echo throughout the space.

It fits my mood to a T.

Cold. Distant. Functional.

I'm sad, but I'm angry, too.

I'm a grown fucking woman, and so little of what has happened to my body so far in this life has been on my own terms.

What happens to me now will *only* happen on my terms.

My body.

My heart.

My soul.

My fucking terms.

I undress stiffly, then get in the shower. Wilson watches me. He slowly follows after grabbing a couple of towels. I hadn't thought of that.

I'm having trouble thinking clearly about anything except this need to be scrubbed clean.

To make my own choices.

The crew stocked the shower with my preferred shampoo and conditioner, so Wilson uses both, and still we don't talk.

There's nothing to say.

He cascades bubbles over my body, shoulders to toes, and massages me everywhere I'm tense.

Still, nothing to say. No break in the cold anger.

When he rinses the conditioner out, it slides slick and smooth down my back, and suddenly I know exactly what I want.

He moves to turn me under the stream, to rinse my back, but I resist and take his hand instead. I show him what I want. I guide his fingers through the slickness to the seam of my ass, then I lean forward and brace my hands against the tile.

He hesitates, his fingertips pressed against my rear entrance.

But he doesn't say anything. I don't want him to. I just want him to take me there, to fill me up and change me. I push back and one fingertip works its way in, violating me by request. I swallow a moan and try to relax. I know how to do this. We've done this before.

"Shhh." He breathes against my ear as he covers my body with his.

I shake my head. No talking.

He sinks his teeth into my neck, a gentle hold, really, but it does the job. It distracts me and then he's inside me, one finger, then two. More liquid dribbles between my cheeks, and he works it into me, pushing me quickly past the uncomfortable burn.

Then his fingers are gone, and the thick cock that replaces them at my entrance is—oh shit, why did I want to do this, oh fuck, no...—pressing into me, and it's so big, it's so hard...

I tip my head back and open my mouth, but nothing comes out. No scream is big enough for this.

And behind me, Wilson is talking now. "Oh, my girl, you're so good. Fucking hell, look at you take me. So pretty. So perfect. I know, I know, it's hard, but you want this. Don't you? You want to chase everything else away, and me too. Fuck. I can't think of anything else right now. Your ass is mine, Tabitha. All mine. You own me, too. You know that? You own my heart."

I push into him, desperate now to have him seated all the way inside me, deep and full and as stretched as I can be.

He leans over me again once he finishes working his cock into me. "Touch yourself," he whispers. "Feel how wet you are. You're dripping onto my balls. You like this? I love it. I love you, too."

Panting, I reach between my legs and he's right. I'm so slick it's on my thighs, and all I have to do is graze my clit and the first tremor of an orgasm threatens.

He swears under his breath. "I felt that inside you, Tabitha. Fucking hell. Do that again."

I stroke a tentative half-circle around my clit and jerk forward against the tile wall from the intensity of it. He follows me, gripping my hips. I start to shake, and he eases out an inch, then pulses back into me. Another thrust, another shivering swipe of my clit. My legs start shaking and I moan his name, then it's all over.

He fucks into me again, and my climax begins. It's unlike anything I've experienced before. I swear it starts in my brain, like an explosion at the base of my skull, then spirals down through my body and wraps around him, deep inside me, triggering more little bombs that go off down my legs, through my belly, and last in my clit, that one so bright and intense that my eyes cross and my words slur together.

Wilson holds me through it, then eases out of me, letting me down to the shower floor. He's still hard and swollen. I watch in awe as he lathers up, then falls to his knees in front of me as he jerks himself hard and fast.

"Where do you want it?" he asks, his eyes bright and fevered.

That's easy. I slither in front of him, and rub my hand over my belly. "Right here," I whisper.

[41]
WILSON

CHICAGO

MARCH

IT'S ALMOST one in the morning by the time I get to the hotel. All I want to do is crawl into bed with Tabitha and crash—hard —but there's still a gauntlet of people to get through in the lobby, and nobody is being allowed up the elevators without a room key. Tabitha's last concert is happening the night before the Democratic primary in Illinois, and Victor Best's campaign has taken over the hotel she's staying at.

I fight through the unexpected crowd to the counter and hand over my identification.

"Wilson Carter," I say. "There's a room key waiting for me."

"Right, yes, there you are, Mr. Carter. Up on the...fifteenth floor. Room 1562. You can take the elevators here to my left."

"Great. Thanks."

I get in the elevator and punch the button for the fifteenth floor, but nothing happens. I push it again, and still nothing. So I try the doors open button, and they do, but then a big, ugly guy wearing an ear piece gets on, and that's like catnip for me. So I don't say anything when he slides his card into the slot at the top of the number panel and pushes the penthouse floor button.

Where Tabitha had been, and was booted from. Which means it's Victor Best's campaign on the top floor. This guy is clearly security, but he doesn't look like Secret Service.

Interesting.

"Floor?" he asks me gruffly.

"I'll go up with you," I say smoothly.

"Not an option."

"Then I'll take fifteen." Can't blame a guy for trying.

"You a reporter?"

"No."

"Why'd you want to come upstairs?"

"To the fifteenth floor?" I play dumb. "That's where I'm staying."

"Are you a registered guest at this hotel?"

"You don't have any right to ask me that."

"You sound like a reporter."

"I'm not." I notice he hasn't pushed the button for my floor, so I lean past him and push all of the buttons. The car jerks to a stop and the doors open. I catch a quick glance that we're on the sixteenth floor before Rambo grabs my arm and pushes me out of the car and up against the opposite wall. "Hey! Watch the face. My girlfriend likes me pretty."

He says something into his radio, and I try to figure out where his feet are. Can I swing a low, sweeping kick and make him fall like a big, ugly oak tree? Bet I can.

Before I get a full chance to weigh the pros and cons of going a few rounds with a presidential candidate's private security guy, a familiar voice tells him to back off.

"Clearly there's been a misunderstanding, right Carter?"

I turn and give Deacon Webb my most innocent smile. "Definitely."

He jerks his head. "Follow me."

"Do you give me orders now?"

He doesn't say anything, and since I'm tiring of being a prick, I do as he asks. He lets us into a room at the end of the hall, next to the stairwell. He leans back against the door.

I start on the offensive. "Who was that guy?"

"None of your business."

"He wasn't Secret Service."

Deacon clenches his jaw and a nerve twitches in his temple. Ah. A sore spot. I'll be sure to poke that again if I need to. "And he's gone. My apologies for the misunderstanding."

"No worries." I reach for the door handle but he doesn't move out of my way.

"Is this a coincidence, you being in Chicago at the same time as Best?"

"Sure it is."

"I *will* arrest you."

"Promises, promises." I wink. "All kidding aside, am I free to go?"

"You're free to answer my questions."

"Then you've de facto arrested me, and I want my lawyer."

Deacon slams his fist against the door. "Fuck off, Carter. You know I'm not going to arrest you. But I need to know what the fuck you're doing here."

"I'm here for a woman." It's a damn cliche, but for once it's the truth. I pace further into the room. "I don't like your protectee, but I promise you, I'm not here about him."

"How did you get a room here?"

"How do I get any hotel room?" I shrug and tap my fingers against an imaginary keyboard. "You should look into their security systems. But actually, I'm seeing someone who already had a room booked here. She's had a...commitment in town for months, booked well in advance, unlike your guy's travel plans."

"What was with the goading on the elevator?"

"Sometimes being reckless gets me results."

"So you do have an agenda."

"Always. But this weekend is about..." I trail off and roll my lower lip between my teeth. Deacon's a good guy. But Tabitha is mine and mine alone. My partners are sworn to secrecy, and as far as her band and crew are concerned, I'm a security consultant. Once Derew/Rook's case is settled, and she can quietly petition a court for an annulment, maybe then we'll let the outside world in. Or maybe never. It's nobody's business but ours what we are to each other.

"A woman." He says it doubtfully.

"It really is."

"I don't believe you. And I don't want to have to shoot you later because you've tried to kill a candidate for the presidency of the United States."

"That was definitely not my plan for the evening."

"I'd feel more comfortable if I knew it wasn't your plan for the year."

I don't plan anything that far out. "I want you to be comfortable with letting me go. I pinky-swear I have no ill intent toward Victor Best or his beautiful young wife."

"What does Ginnifer have to do with this?" His voice hardens, and I don't miss it.

I give him a slow appraisal. "She's friends with Tabitha Leyton. I think you've probably met Tabitha, yes?"

He nods. "They had dinner tonight." Understanding dawns, and he rocks back on his heels. "Vegas. That was you?"

Another nod.

"Tabitha's nice."

"Hands off."

He laughs. "Okay." He moves out of the way. "Have a nice night, Carter. See you around."

I take the stairs down to the floor below, where my love is waiting.

She swings the door open as I approach. "There's my secret girl," I whisper as she folds into my arms.

"I've missed you." She tips her face up to mine and I dip her back so we can kiss.

"I'm going to quit my job and follow your tour like a groupie."

"Luckily it ends tomorrow night, because I think you like your job." She kisses my jaw. "Come to bed."

"In a minute." I dump my bag on the luggage rack and pull out the long, flat jewelry box from the front pocket. "I got you something to celebrate the end of the tour. And the start of us."

The box opens smoothly. Inside is a long, narrow gold chain with a heart in the middle.

"It's a belly chain," I explain, suddenly unsure if it's a good gift or not. It made sense when I bought it. "And the heart can sit..."

She blinks up at me, her eyes swimming brightly with unshed tears. "I get it. Oh, Wilson. I love it. I love you. It's perfect."

I kneel in front of her and she lifts her t-shirt, baring herself to me. I wind the chain around her waist, carefully connecting the clasps first before resting the pendant right above the filigree heart at the bottom of her tattoo.

It is perfect.

ONE YEAR LATER

SEATTLE

FEBRUARY

MY SECRET GIRL has the flu. She's been sick for days, and I've been playing nursemaid—and a few rounds of dirty doctor, too.

Even when she's not feeling well, we still slide into that desperate, needy connection that was all that we had for so long.

I glance around the waiting room. Her new doctor has been extraordinarily good with her, patient and understanding.

The door from the clinic space opens and Tabitha steps out. She's still talking to the nurse. "Still keep taking the Tylenol?"

"Yes, that's fine. Lots of rest, fluids, and making sure you're eating enough, that's the main thing."

"Will do."

"And we'll see you back here in another month."

I stand up and hold her coat for her as she wriggles her arms into it. "Ready to go?"

She gives me an unexpected grin. "I am. There's a quick stop we need to make on the way home."

I'd gotten a perfect parking spot, so my Range Rover is right out front. I still have my Tesla in Washington, but I needed something more rugged for out here, and the Rover was just as compatible with the electronic upgrades I'd gotten used to in my Tesla.

The security system at her house—our house—for example, is fully integrated into the car. I can pull up all the same video streams I can on my phone, even take a snapshot with the touch of my finger and send it to my bots to run through the databases.

Bulletproof glass, reinforced doors...the only thing it's missing is a rocket launcher.

Washington State frowns on those in cars, and I'm trying to be more law-abiding these days.

Today I just need the built-in wifi to find— "Where are we stopping?"

"A drugstore." She covers my hand with hers. Her fingers are cool, and I lift them to my lips to warm them up. That's when I realize she's shaking.

I lift my eyes to her face. "What is it?"

"I need prenatal vitamins," she whispers. "I'm pregnant."

Time to take another step into the light.

THE END
(for now)

———

———

Ginnifer and Deacon's story, First Lady, will come after the Forbidden Bodyguards series ends. Get on my VIP Reader mailing list and join my Facebook group to keep in touch if you want to be in the loop!

The Forbidden Bodyguards Series

Hate F*@k (Cole and Hailey)
Booty Call (Ali and Scott)
Dirty Love (Wilson and Tabitha)
Wicked Sin (Taylor and Luke)
Filthy Liar (Jason and Melinda)

www.ainsleybooth.com

the **Frisky Beavers** series

co-written with Sadie Haller

Prime Minister

Dr. Bad Boy

Full Mountie

Mr. Hat Trick

Page of Swords

Bull of the Woods

the **Pine Harbour** series

writing as Zoe York

Love in a Small Town

Love in a Snow Storm

Love on a Spring Morning

Love on a Summer Night

Love on the Run

Love in a Sandstorm

Love on the Outskirts of Town

ACKNOWLEDGMENTS

Sadie Haller has a permanent spot at the top of my thank you list, because she's always there to read and share brain waves and wield a red pen.

Another constant is Jessica Alcazar, who runs my reader group and puts up with a daily barrage of new shiny ideas from me. Thank you for putting up with all the butterfly moments!

My friend Rachel, who was the first person to read my first book ever, weighed in on a technical question for this book. There's something really special about a friend that still thinks it's cool you're writing a book the thirtieth time round.

Much thanks also goes to Lori, who has endless patience for my distractions. Thank you for just quietly taking care of things while I dream.

And of course, always, always, always I appreciate my Vikings, the big one and the little ones, for being patient as I write and edit and design. Tomorrow we'll go see Lego Batman.

~ Ainsley

www.ainsleybooth.com

ABOUT THE AUTHOR

Ainsley Booth is a USA Today bestselling author of more than fifty romances between this pen name and her alter-ego, Zoe York. She lives in London, Ontario, Canada with her family.

facebook.com/ainsleyboothwrites

instagram.com/ainsleyboothwrites

www.ingramcontent.com/pod-product-compliance
Lightning Source LLC
Chambersburg PA
CBHW031009190726